Red Spy at Night

Red Spy at Night

by

Helga Pohl-Wannenmacher

A True Story of Espionage and Seduction
behind the Iron Curtain

Translated by
Rena Wilson

Leo Cooper · London

First published in this edition in
Great Britain in 1978 by
Leo Cooper Ltd,
196 Shaftesbury Avenue,
London WC2H 8JL

ISBN 0 85052 220 X

Printed and bound in Great Britain by
REDWOOD BURN LIMITED
Trowbridge & Esher

Contents

PART THREE

Prologue

The Lubianka! That name is known everywhere, in Moscow, in the Soviet Union, throughout the world. The new prisoner, following a warder along the corridor, knew it too. But she had not imagined that the notorious prison would be so quiet, so sterile. The corridor was equipped with traffic lights, like a city street. When a light turned red, the prisoner had to stop and stand with her face to the wall. Then she would hear the sound of footsteps behind her. When they had passed, the light would turn green again and she would be allowed to proceed. Prisoners must never see each other.

She was wearing an earth-coloured jacket and trousers, men's uniform from Soviet Army supplies. They looked absurd on a woman in her seventh month of pregnancy. The reception staff had taken away her own clothes and given her these dreadful things. After that, her particulars had been entered in the Iron Register No. 2 of the Lubianka: Jelena Kirilovna Pushkova, born 1927, married to Andrei Sidrov, Colonel in the Soviet Army. Throughout the committal procedures, she had thought of Andrei and of his child she was expecting, and she had longed for food and sleep, if only for the baby's sake.

Now, on her way to be interrogated, she put food and sleep out of her mind and tried to concentrate on what she could safely say, and what she must not. She knew that if they beat her, she would tell everything – but surely they never beat women in her condition?

9

The warder stopped at Room No. 656. There was a green light above the door. The prisoner was led into a bright room comfortably furnished with armchairs, two settees and a polished desk. From the wall, comrade Stalin looked down, fatherly.

They did not beat her. They set a meal before her such as she had not seen for a long time – soup, roast chicken, white bread, brown bread, butter, jam, oranges, grapes and honey-coloured cake. And in the Ukraine there was famine . . .

But she was not allowed to eat yet. The oldest of the KGB men came up to her. He had red hair, red eyebrows, green eyes. He addressed her kindly, like a benevolent uncle.

'Child, you are still so young, and so pretty, too. It would be a shame if we had to keep you here for long.'

She said nothing.

'Now, why don't you admit that you were working for the Americans?'

'I have never worked for the Americans,' she said, and that was the truth.

'You were caught trying to cross the border. No loyal Soviet citizen would do that. Why don't you admit that you had a reason to escape?'

'No, I wasn't trying to escape,' she said, and that was a lie. The KGB man gently shook his head and adjusted the tray in front of her. The prisoner covered her face with her hands so that she need not see the food. But the voice went on.

'The truth, comrade, tell us the truth now!'

Part One

CHAPTER ONE

Divided Loyalties

The truth, I thought. Where would I have to start? Jelena Pushkova is not my name. I am not Russian. Nor am I really German, if I think back far enough. My name is Helga Wannenmacher and until I was twelve years old I lived in Deliatin, in Galicia, where my parents and grandparents had lived before me. We were comfortably off; my father owned a sawmill, there were farms and a saltmine in the family, and I had a happy, sheltered childhood.

The German invasion of Poland in 1939 ended it overnight. Because the Wannenmachers had come from Germany originally, my brother Jossi and I were boycotted, even by our friends, with the pitiless logic of children. At first, the adults suffered less. Father's employees remained loyal, and, indeed, looked to him for guidance – which he could not give.

Later, when Poland was partitioned between Russia and Germany, Deliatin lay in the Russian zone and our sawmill was declared public property. Father was forbidden to enter it; the timber and the machinery were sent to Russia and so was everything of value on the farms, including my own pony. Life under socialism would have been intolerable for my parents: the decision to leave was made for them by a compulsory repatriation of German nationals to the Reich.

Jossi and I were secretly rather excited about this, though the move was brutally done. Women and children were sent by train, the men in trucks, and the baggage allowance was

11

twenty-five kilos per person. Mother simply couldn't accept the fact that all our silver and valuables would be left behind. She spent the last few days scrubbing the house from top to bottom, 'for when we come back', and as we finally left, on Christmas Day, she locked everything as carefully as if we were just going on a visit.

Mother and I spent several fretful weeks in a repatriation camp just across the border, waiting for Father and Jossi to join us. It was late February by the time they arrived, and after that things started looking up. Father got on the telephone and soon had us all moved to Strehlen, a small town twenty-five miles from Breslau, where we began our new life.

At first school was a worse ordeal than it had been in Deliatin after the invasion. There, I had been 'The German'; here I was 'The Pole'. My German was not very good, I couldn't follow the lessons, and I was bullied by teachers and pupils alike. But the humiliation didn't last long – thanks to a natural ability to run and jump! Like everyone else, I had to join the 'Girls' Hitler Youth', which at that time was chiefly concerned with athletics, and this was one field in which I could easily outshine my tormentors. I soon became the local champion and Group Sports Leader, and my faulty German was quite forgotten.

The following year, I was selected to take part in the National Youth Contest in Berlin, where I won the long-jump. Hitler himself came to address us, and I had a good view of him from only a short distance away. It was all tremendously thrilling.

*

On 22 June, 1941, Germany declared war on the Soviet Union, and I was told to start learning Russian. I already spoke Polish and Ukrainian, my German was by now quite good, and interpreters would be needed in a Reich that was going to extend to the Urals. Then I was offered a place at a special boarding school run and paid for by the State. Besides athletics and the domestic arts, its thirty-five privileged students underwent a thorough political indoctrination; we were being groomed as the élite of Nazi womanhood. Discipline was strict, and we had to work hard, but – apart from the politics, which we all found boring – it was a marvellous education received in surroundings of considerable luxury. When the year's course was over I couldn't face going back to an ordinary school. I joined the Red Cross and divided my time between the dispensary at Strehlen Military Hospital, the Girls' Hitler Youth and my Russian studies.

In the autumn Jossi came on leave from the Eastern Front, very depressed in spite of his Iron Cross and his promotion to corporal in the Luftwaffe, which he had joined while I was away at school. He had been to Deliatin on his way home, and brought us the first news of the massacre of Jews that was going on all over Poland. In the woods above the sawmill where we had played as children he had actually witnessed the shooting of many of our friends, and he couldn't get the horror of it out of his mind. He didn't want to see anybody and just sat in his room, more or less in a state of shock. Nothing would induce him to return to his unit when his leave was up, and he spent some days hiding in the hayloft above our stables. Eventually, of course, the military police caught up with him, but thanks to an influential friend of ours, Herr Cramm, who had a word with someone, Jossi wasn't courtmartialled.

Over the next eighteen months, optimism about the Russian front began to fade, and the effects of the war became noticeable even in Strehlen. Evacuees poured in from the bombed cities; the shops had little to sell, and the queues grew longer. In January, 1945, the Soviet army advanced into Silesia, and, in spite of Party orders for everyone to stay where they were, refugees began fleeting westward.

The Wannenmacher family was among them. Herr Cramm had property in Güsten and invited us to go there with him. It was a terrible journey. The weather was bitterly cold and the roads were choked with frightened people, and with military convoys trying to get through to the east. Once, we had to lie in a ditch while enemy aircraft flew over and strafed us; afterwards the snow was stained with blood.

In Güsten, however, life went on much as before. I did voluntary work at the hospital, joined the local branch of the Girls' Hitler Youth and trained for the athletic club's Sports Day. A few bombs fell on the town. Defeat was in the air, and everyone knew that the war must end soon. The official Party

line still maintained that victory was just around the corner;
the German people were more realistic. But it was spring, I
was almost eighteen, Herr Cramm kept assuring me I was
pretty – and I had an unprofessional tendency to fall in love
with my patients at the hospital.

*

Then the Americans arrived and the war was over. At first the
collapse of Germany didn't affect me much. I was in love, as
usual, and the weather was glorious. My first brush with the
conquerors came while I was swimming in the river with my
friends Gerda and Adelheid. We had raced each other to the
bridge and were bobbing about under it when some American
soldiers ordered us out of the water, bundled us into a jeep,
and took us, all dripping wet as we were, to the nearest command post. They insisted that we had been trying to blow up
the bridge, and it was some time before a charming staff sergeant called Bob Kelly managed to convince everyone of our
harmlessness. When we were released he drove us back to the
river to collect our clothes and then took each of us home. I
was last and before he put me down he asked if he might see me
again.

The next evening he came back in a freshly-laundered uniform to call on Father, pretending that he had been sent by
his captain to apologize for the incident at the bridge. Afterwards Father called him a very likeable man.

'How can you, Karl! He's an American!' Mother reproached
him.

'So what? We mustn't hang on to these national prejudices.
Many Americans are of German origin anyway.'

Bob Kelly was not of German origin, but he was very
methodical and called on Father often when he was passing in
his jeep. As intended, I came to look forward to these visits,
and soon realized that the broad-shouldered Bob with his black
moustache was much more interesting than my current boy-
friend.

'An excellent man, this Mr Kelly,' Father remarked, and he
didn't mind Bob taking me for a walk occasionally, though
Mother wasn't so keen. She believed that a young girl ought
to be home by seven o'clock sharp; but there was always Aunt

Lisa in Alsleben, who had more liberal attitudes and was happy for me to stay with her whenever I liked. These visits quickly became a regular thing. I would bicycle to the edge of town where Bob would be waiting in the jeep; we'd put the bike in the back and go off somewhere for the day.

Gerda and Adelheid also lived in Alsleben, so if necessary I could tell Aunt Lisa that I'd stayed with them. All too soon it was necessary. Bob took me to a party at another unit; we danced a lot and drank a lot, and when we left it was very late indeed. Bob was thoughtful enough to book me into a hotel so that I need not risk catching cold on the drive back in an open car. And he was considerate enough not to leave me alone in that unfamiliar room.

In the morning I cried with repentance and Bob reassured me.

'What is there to cry about, honey? We'll get married, of course we will!' He told me many other pretty things too, including how glad he was that he would have a German wife. He even asked Father for my hand.

'My dear Mr Kelly,' Father laughed, 'the child is just eighteen! Wait another year and then we can talk about it again.' Bob and I had to be satisfied with that.

But in those days everything turned out differently from what one had planned. Not long after this interview, Bob arrived in his jeep much earlier than usual. He was in a tearing hurry; the Americans were going to Berlin and the Russians were taking over. He begged me to persuade the family to move to Berlin so that we could be together again; then with a squeal of tyres he was gone.

We discussed what to do. We were all frightened of the Russians, but Mother was ill in bed. Could we really pack everything up and flee again? No, the Wannenmachers had had enough, and, in spite of Bob, I didn't want to go to Berlin by myself.

So the Americans left and the Russians arrived. Everybody stayed at home, uncertain what to expect. At midnight there was a knock on our front door; the Mayor's wife was outside with a Soviet soldier: I was to go to the town hall because the Russians needed an interpreter. Father absolutely refused to

let me go, and I bitterly regretted having learnt Russian. The
Mayor's wife pleaded:

'Please, do reconsider, Herr Wannenmacher! What am I to
do? Do you want Helga to be fetched by force?'

The soldier was showing signs of impatience. Father made
a decision.

'Tell him, only on condition that I can come too.' Haltingly,
I translated. The Russian nodded quite calmly.

'Da, da,' he said, 'davai, davai!' That meant 'quickly', and it
was the first time I heard a Russian say the word. Later I was
to learn to hate it.

The Mayor's office was crowded with people and there was
a strong smell of Russian cigarettes. An officer with two stars
on his shoulder straps asked me if I spoke Russian.

'Yes, but not very well.'

'Okay, let's try it. We need a large house for the command
post.'

I consulted with Father and the Mayor. They agreed to offer
them the building formerly occupied by the District Party
Council. I translated, and the officer smiled as he thanked me.
He didn't really look as though he could hurt anybody.

'By the way,' he said, 'your Russian is excellent! You may
go now. Thank you very much.'

Father was grumbling all the way home.

'I don't like it, I don't like it at all. Now they'll send for you
every time they need an interpreter. It's too dangerous.' He
paused. 'I tell you what! You go to Alsleben and stay with
Aunt Lisa. And don't tell anybody you speak Russian, you
hear!'

I rather liked this idea. In Alsleben, I worked at the chemist's
shop. There wasn't much to do because stocks of medicines
had long since been used up and new supplies were scarce. The
Russians didn't seem to be bad at all. Stalin had decreed that
any soldier who raped a German girl was to be sentenced to
ten years' hard labour in Siberia. And they didn't declare
everything public property as they had in Deliatin. Even Herr
Cramm, the former Party official, was allowed to go on manag-
ing his estates. Reassured, I ventured home one week-end.

My mare Hanka needed exercise and I thought there would
be no harm in riding her around the country lanes. But I was

wrong. I encountered a troop of Russian soldiers who, assuming in spite of my protests that I was a wealthy landowner, forced me to dismount and then locked me and Hanka in a garage. We were left there for five hours and then I was taken to the commandant.

His name was written on the door of his office: Andrei Sidrov, Lieutenant-Colonel. I recognized him immediately; he was the officer for whom I had translated at the town hall.

'What a nice surprise,' he smiled. 'Wherever have you been hiding? We've been looking for you for weeks.'

'What do you want from me?' I felt bold enough to ask him. 'And what are you going to do with my horse? You won't slaughter it, will you?'

'Slaughter your horse? What do you take us for? We're not short of meat. You must have been having your leg pulled. By the way, have you eaten?'

I had to admit that I was very hungry. An orderly brought food – herrings with vodka followed by roast beef and vegetables. It was my first Russian meal, and it was very good indeed, but I was in a hurry to get home and didn't finish it.

The commandant had his car brought round and drove me back himself. Later, a freshly-groomed Hanka was brought to the house by a soldier. Next day the commandant paid an official call on my father to ask if I might work as an interpreter at the command post. Father frowned.

'Think about it,' the Russian suggested, 'I'll ask again tomorrow.' Then he took his leave.

He had made a good impression. 'Surprisingly pleasant manners,' Father said. 'It just goes to show, there are human beings among the Russians, too.'

The matter was discussed by the family. Herr Cramm advised us to accept the offer; he could see the advantages.

'As an interpreter,' he said, 'the child will have more influence with the commandant than anyone else.' Next day Father gave his consent.

Herr Cramm was quite right. I soon became a well-known and influential personality in Güsten. Colonel Sidrov was an energetic man whose job was to create order out of the turmoil left by the war. Shops were reopened, factories put back into production, even local politics began to flourish again. And there was not one application that I did not translate and put to the commandant; no petitioner who did not speak first to me, whether the matter concerned a travel permit or an enquiry about a prisoner-of-war. In public I was always at the commandant's side. 'Jelena,' he called me, because my second Christian name in Helen, and Helga is too difficult for a Russian to pronounce. I called him 'comrade Commandant'.

Eventually Bob heard about what was going on. One afternoon he arrived at the office in his immaculate uniform with breast pockets bulging with Lucky Strikes and candy packs. He kissed me, highly amused.

'Honey, I thought you were frightened of the Russians!'

'Oh, they aren't so bad,' I eagerly assured him. 'I think it was all propaganda. And the commandant is really very nice!'

The American staff-sergeant and the Russian lieutenant-colonel took a liking to each other. I was given permission to invite them both home for the evening, and we celebrated with vodka and whisky. When Bob left, he embraced the commandant and kissed him on both cheeks in the Russian manner. At the door he whispered to me: 'They're just like us, aren't they?'

CHAPTER TWO

Unwelcome Advances

There was one important difference. The Russians had a security officer and the Americans had not. In Güsten it was Major Jatshuk. Nobody at the post liked him because his job consisted mainly of spying on everyone else. Jatshuk worked closely with the German communists; one evening I saw a list that he had put on the commandant's desk:

'The following persons are known to be dangerous fascists, militarists or subversive elements, and are recommended for transfer to the USSR.'

Fifteen names and addresses were listed under that ominous heading, and I knew three of them, two men and one woman. They were nice, harmless citizens who wouldn't hurt a fly. I memorized the names and told my father about it. He said nothing. Two days later it became known in Güsten that overnight twelve people had been arrested and taken away. Three others had escaped to the West shortly before.

I felt a secret triumph. One could help people out of a tight corner if one worked at the command post! I could hardly wait for a chance to do it again. I wasn't frightened of the Russians any more, not even of Major Jatshuk. Being so close to the commandant, I felt safe; he was a real gentleman. I liked him, and I was not unaware that he liked me too.

Unfortunately, Major Jatshuk seemed to have his eye on me as well. I couldn't stand him, quite apart from his odious spying job. He was coarse, uncouth and totally unattractive. But he often asked me to accompany him on official business, and every time I refused he winked and said, 'Of course, you'd much rather stay with your beloved commandant, wouldn't you, my dear?'

Jatshuk wasn't far wrong. I would have fallen in love with the commandant long ago had it not been for Bob.

Once, I couldn't get out of going; Lieutenant-Colonel Sidrov himself ordered it. It was a long trip and the major was in the best of moods. He became quite expansive and told me all about his home town in the Ukraine and how good life was there, how respected an officer of the Soviet Army was, and how, following the Russian victory, great times were about to come for all Soviet people.

We passed a peasant's garden where an old man was picking cherries. Jatshuk stopped the car and bought a whole basketful. We sat down by the roadside and ate them.

'Jelena,' Jatshuk began, skilfully spitting the stones into the road, 'Jelena, you are a woman who would fit in well in the Soviet Union. It would be a pity if you were to stay in this country – it's finished.' And then he put his arms round me and drew me towards him. I had been expecting something of the sort and quickly wriggled free and jumped up. Jatshuk grabbed me round the waist.

'What's the matter, little love? I'm not doing you any harm!'

I pushed with the edge of my hand against his adam's apple and he let go of me so suddenly that I fell straight into the basket. My best suit was ruined. When he tried to embrace me again I really lost my temper and hit him hard across the face. That finally was enough for him; he let me go and wiped his face. The old man in the garden chuckled with spiteful pleasure. Jatshuk noticed him and went white with rage.

'You will regret that, you bitch!' he said hoarsely. 'Come on, we have work to do.'

I thought no more about it.

*

That autumn, the commandant had business in Berlin and he offered to take me with him. It was a chance to see Bob and I jumped at it. The visit was an eye-opener. Bob seemed pleased enough to see me, but it was soon clear that he wasn't missing me at all. He had another girlfriend and our romance – if such it had ever been – was over.

The commandant was extraordinarily sympathetic. I cried a bit on his shoulder, and he kissed my forehead in a fatherly manner. Then he took me out and bought me presents, and in the car going back to Güsten he kissed me again – properly. The German driver was watching in the mirror and at once it was all over town that we were having an affair. But I didn't care. I was in love again!

Sidrov was very correct. He would talk to me about himself and his family, and he encouraged me to call him Andrei when we were alone, but he seldom even kissed me and I felt as safe with him as I had always done. So I didn't hesitate when he invited me to his flat one evening.

Of course we spent the night together, but in the morning I didn't cry. Andrei proposed there and then.

'I am twelve years older than you are, Jelena, but I want you to be my wife. Will you marry me?'

The difference in age wasn't important, but how could a Soviet Army colonel marry a German girl? Stalin would never allow it.

'I'll arrange that somehow,' Andrei promised. 'So what do you say, Jelena?'

Before I could answer, there was a knock on the door.

'Who is it?' Andrei called.

'It's Major Jatshuk, comrade Commandant. The interpreter's father is here. He is looking for his daughter.'

Andrei hesitated only for a second. 'The interpreter Jelena stayed at her aunt's house in Alsleben last night.'

'Please forgive the disturbance, comrade Commandant.'

A few days later, Andrei was summoned before the Supreme Command in Potsdam. He said he would apply for a marriage permit at the same time; and when he came back, grave and drawn, I assumed only that permission had been refused. But it was much worse than that. Major Jatshuk had denounced his commandant for living with a German woman – me, and associating with an American – Bob. Andrei was recalled to Moscow and Jatshuk was appointed commandant in his place.

We said goodbye in Andrei's office.

'Will you write to me?' My voice was choked with tears.

21

'No, I'm afraid that won't be possible.'

'But will we never see each other again?'

'Oh Jelena, who knows? I shall do everything I can to come back here, but it won't be easy.'

I stood at the window and watched him get into the car. Jatshuk accompanied him outside and saluted as the car moved off. Andrei did not return the salute, and, within seconds, the man I so desperately wanted to marry was swallowed by the grey November fog.

*

I cried all night, and in the morning I handed in my resignation.

'But this is a great shame!' Jatshuk looked at me kindly. 'You are such an efficient interpreter. Won't you think it over?'

'Of course not – and you know perfectly well why!' I stormed out of the command post; I never wanted to see Jatshuk again or Güsten either; everything reminded me of Andrei.

I went to work at the hospital dispensary in Alsleben. After I had been there about a fortnight, Jossi came over.

'Helga, you must come home at once! Father has been arrested!'

We hurried back together and I went immediately to Jatshuk, who was all smiles.

'Well, well, look who's here! I thought you must have gone over to the West.'

'Is that why you've arrested my father?'

'Oh, that was only so that he could help us with our enquiries. I had to find out where you had gone, you see. You were a bad security risk.'

I choked down my disgust and told Jatshuk where I was working. 'You can verify that with a simple telephone call. Now, will you release my father?'

'Why, of course I will!' The new commandant smiled sweetly. 'I would suggest, however, that you come back to work for us as an interpreter. That would be better for you, better for us and, believe me, very much better for your father.'

So there was no alternative, and on the whole it wasn't as bad as I'd expected. Major Jatshuk was unbelievably friendly and generous. Food was scarce in that famine winter of 1946, but the Wannenmacher family didn't suffer. The biggest surprise of all was that Jatshuk no longer tried to kiss me, although he had become the absolute ruler of Güsten.

The German communists were busy supplying lists of suspected fascists, and once again I memorized the names I knew and passed them on to Father. Sometimes the warning system worked and sometimes it didn't, but nobody could prove that I was involved.

One day I found Miss Petzold's name on the list. She was an elderly dressmaker who occasionally did some sewing for me. The very idea of her having anything to do with politics was so preposterous that, without thinking, I went straight to Jatshuk.

'I can assure you, comrade Commandant, this woman has never done a harmful thing in her whole life!'

Jatshuk smiled and winked. 'Hasn't she, now? Women are never harmless in my experience. Just look at you, for example!'

I managed to ignore this. 'Miss Petzold doesn't even know what a fascist is!'

Jatshuk got up and came towards me. 'Really?'

'Really, comrade Commandant!'

He put his loathsome, hairy hands on my shoulders and clasped me to him. He kissed me on both cheeks, and I didn't resist. Then he let go of me, took a pencil and crossed Miss Petzold's name off the list.

Eventually the name I had been dreading appeared – Otto Cramm. I had to save him. He had been such a good friend to us all – and he had also been a high-ranking official of the Nazi Party. I went to Jatshuk and swore blind that Herr Cramm was no fascist.

'Really?'

'Really, comrade Commandant!'

This time, to make quite certain, I returned his kiss.

*

All that winter the purge of 'fascist and subversive elements' went on, and a great round-up was planned for Christmas Day. One hundred and sixty families were to be arrested, but, when the police went for them, sixteen had already fled. The local Party secretary came storming into the command post and told Jatshuk that I had warned them.

'Did you, Jelena? Tell me the truth. You know I shall get to it anyway.'

'I've never warned anyone,' I said – and this was true as far as it went. 'I may have talked too much; if so, I'm sorry.'

The commandant's expression was difficult to interpret. He stared at me; then he went to the window and stood looking out into the darkness, without saying anything. I thought of the trouble my father would be in if anyone found out that he had warned the families, and involuntarily I started to cry. Jatshuk turned round.

'You will come to my flat tonight at eight. Nobody must see you. Then we can discuss how to get you out of this mess.'

I arrived punctually. The major had taken off his jacket and opened the door in his braces. On the table stood a bottle of vodka and two glasses. The flat had once been Andrei's and everything in it reminded me of him.

I wouldn't drink with Jatshuk, so he drank alone. He sat pressed against me on the sofa.

'I have been thinking about the problem,' he began. 'You really have got yourself into serious trouble!'

It didn't seem worth answering, because I knew that he could get me out of it if he wanted to; he was not only the commandant but also the security officer; his word would be accepted in Potsdam. Jatshuk interrupted my thoughts.

'There is one way to save you – we must get married!'

I was so appalled that I could only stammer, 'But that's impossible, you know that! I'm not a Russian citizen.'

Jatshuk laughed. 'For me, everything is possible. I'll make a Russian citizen of you in no time at all.' He turned to embrace me.

'Oh please, not now!'

'Why not, dammit?'

I fought him off, knowing that I was breaking the rules, that it was time to pay for Miss Petzold, and for Otto Cramm, and to make a down payment on my own freedom. But in that room where Andrei and I had loved each other, I just couldn't do it.

At last Jatshuk got up, poured himself another vodka, lit a cigarette, and was suddenly quite calm again.

'Jelena, nobody can treat me like that, you know. But, damn you, I love it! I think you've got character; I've got character

24

too. That's why we are suited. You will find out how very well suited we are! Think about it. We can get married and everything will be fine. You have all night to decide. And now you can go – if you want to.'

He accompanied me to the door. Before I left, he lightly stroked my hair.

'Don't be dumb, girl!' He said it like a true friend.

CHAPTER THREE

Ten years' Hard Labour

I told Father everything, and the only solution he could think of was that I should escape to Berlin. It was a cold night; I dressed in my riding habit, threw a few things into a case, and set off on my bicycle towards Magdeburg, where I could catch a train.

It was getting light and I was nearly there when a military vehicle pulled up in front of me and two soldiers got out and asked for my papers. I still had the interpreter's card with Andrei's signature. The Russians took it, glanced at it briefly and pointed to the car: 'Get in!'

For two days and two nights I sat in Magdeburg military prison, in solitary confinement. Nobody interrogated me, nobody took any notice of me, except that coffee was brought in the morning and soup at midday, both tasting much the same. On the third morning there were different footsteps in the corridor; the door was opened and Major Jatshuk entered my cell.

'Hallo, Jelena!'

'Hallo, comrade Major.'

He sat down on the bed. 'Did you really think it was that easy?'

I didn't bother to answer.

'You were going to Berlin, weren't you? To that American fellow?'

I nodded. Then he repeated all his old threats and promises.

I only had to marry him and everything would be fine. He had me moved to a comfortable cell with curtains and a proper bed, and he came to me there in the middle of the night.

'I want to give you a last chance,' he murmured. 'You can be free tomorrow; it's up to you.'

I shook my head wearily. Then he was on top of me and tearing at my clothes. When his awful hands touched my breasts, I pushed my thumb into his eye as hard as I could. He screamed with pain and threw me on the floor.

'Damn you, you fascist whore! You'll be sorry for this!'

Cursing, he left the room and locked the door – and that was the last time I ever saw him.

Next morning I was taken to Potsdam prison where I was interrogated every day for a fortnight. I was accused of having betrayed official secrets, of having aided and abetted capitalists and former fascists in their flight to the West, of having attempted to defect to the West myself, and of having had secret dealings with the Americans. I denied all the charges over and over again, but it was no use. Bob's letters were lying on the table as 'proof', so they must have searched our house. Had they arrested Father again? I had no way of finding out.

On 10 January, 1946, at four o'clock in the afternoon, without ever having been brought to trial, I was told the verdict.

'In accordance with paragraph 56, sections 4, 6 and 10 of the Criminal Code, you, Helga Helen Angelika Wannenmacher, are sentenced to serve a term of hard labour in a penal camp in Siberia. There you will be given the opportunity to make up for the crimes you have committed against the Soviet Union. Term of imprisonment: 10 years.'

At eighteen it sounded like a life sentence. I was shocked and stunned, and for the next few days I hardly noticed what was happening to me. I was taken from Potsdam to Berlin in a trance of misery and put into an air-raid shelter to wait, with some twenty other women, for the next stage in our degradation.

Near me was a pretty girl of about my own age. She told me she was a dancer, she came from Dresden and her name was Brigitte Muller.

'How many years did you get?' she asked.

'Ten.'

'That seems to be their standard term. Are you political?'

I nodded. 'Are you political too?'

'I don't know if you could call it that. I danced the can-can in our variety show.'

'So what?'

'Oh, you know the can-can. At the end you turn round and raise your skirts to show the audience your bottom.'

'What's wrong with that?'

'Well, you tell me! The Russians in the audience thought the dance was provocative, so they arrested me. I was interrogated for days until they found out that I had danced occasionally in the American sector of Berlin. So they did me for collaborating with the Americans and insulting Soviet soldiers. Boy! Ten years in Siberia for one can-can.'

The iron door was pushed open and we were ordered over to the delousing station.

'All of us?' an old lady indignantly asked. She had rouge on her withered cheeks and was wearing a fur coat.

'Of course all of you! We can do without German bugs and lice in the Soviet Union.'

'This is incredible!' the old lady cried. 'Are you suggesting that I have . . . '

'Shut up!'

There was silence. We were all mortally afraid of the wardress. From the delousing station, we were taken to the barber.

'Now we are going to be shorn.' One of the women knew what it was all about.

'Completely?' The old lady in the fur coat touched her waved silvery hair.

'Like billiard balls.' The knowledgeable one laughed miserably.

I hung back at the end of the queue, but there was no escape, and at last I was pushed into the room. The floor was covered with hair – white, grey, blonde and brown in all shades imaginable. My eyes filled with tears.

'There, there,' a woman in a white coat consoled, 'it doesn't hurt, you know. How old are you, love? You don't look more than sixteen! What have you done?'

I told her and she listened with interest. 'Ten years, well, that's not too bad.'

'Don't you think so? I'll be twenty-eight when I come back!'
'That's nothing! There was one here earlier who got twenty-five years – and she's fifty. She'll be lucky if she lives to get out.'
'And you, how long did you get?'
'Oh, I'm not a prisoner,' the woman said cheerfully. 'I'm civilian personnel, so they tell me. I got the job by way of compensation.'
'Compensation for what?'
'They raped me. Sixteen times in one night. When they're drunk, there's nothing you can do to stop them. Anyway there were always two holding me down. I was in hospital for three weeks afterwards. Then an officer came and apologized and when I got out they gave me this job. It's all right. Breakfast, lunch, supper – everything free and large helpings, too. On top of that, they even pay me wages!'

Another colour was added to the heap on the floor. Finally the woman held up a mirror and I burst into tears.
'It'll grow again, dear,' she said. 'That's the only thing you can count on.' She glanced towards the door, and then gave me a piece of paper and a pencil.
'Quick, write a line to your parents. I'll post it for you.'
I told them where I was going and said I was all right. My tears were dripping on to the paper. The woman picked up a curl of my hair to go with the message.

*

The journey to Siberia took about two months. It was difficult to keep track of time; there were frequent interminable stops, and our goods train sometimes spent up to a week in a siding while more important trains went through. The cattle trucks in which we lived were intolerably crowded at first; but, as a guard sardonically remarked, 'Some of you will soon make room for the others.' Nearly half of us did. The first to go was the old lady in the fur coat. Her body was thrown out into the snow; her coat was kept.

All through Germany and Poland our rations consisted of two buckets of hot water a day – 'kipyatok', the guards called it. Once we were over the border into Russia there was food of a sort, cabbage soup. Several women died of it after the long diet of water.

29

Eventually our train stopped in the middle of nowhere. The survivors were off-loaded, packed into lorries and driven for four hours over the icy tundra. At dusk we reached the camp. Stiff and cold, we shuffled through the gate to the reception hut where our names were registered and we were each given a mess tin, a mug and a wooden spoon. Then we were marched off to the women's compound.

The atmosphere in hut 17 almost took our breath away. All the windows were closed, a stove in the middle of the dim room gave off an incredible heat, and the stench of some seventy women hit us like a fist. They were sitting or standing around, half-naked, staring at us with curious eyes. For a moment no one spoke. Then from the darkness at the back of the hut a truly gross creature came forward; her body was covered with tattooing and she had a voice like a rasp.

'Who are you? Where do you come from?'

I was the only one who could understand the questions, so I answered for the others. The fat woman grinned.

'From Germany, eh? I see – fascist whores!'

I began to protest.

'Shut your face, you bitch!' The tattooed monstrosity came nearer. 'I'm the *starosta* and you'd better learn to do as I tell you right away. Or you'll soon find out what happens to people who don't!'

The word 'starosta' meant something like 'barrack chief'. I explained the situation to the rest of our party who were still crowding silently by the entrance.

'Line up against the wall over there!' the starosta commanded. She had now been joined by several other equally repulsive women. 'Put down your things and get undressed!'

The German prisoners obeyed. Naked, we stood in front of the starosta and her bodyguards; we didn't resist while our scanty possessions were looted; silk panties, brassieres, slips and fur coats changed hands. Finally, we were told to put our clothes on again and find ourselves bunks, while our tormentors withdrew to the back of the hut.

'One other thing!' shouted the starosta, 'this part is out of bounds. Anyone who comes back here will be beaten. Understand?'

We heard them arguing over the loot, and then a high, sharp

voice silenced them and issued some orders. Presently the starosta reappeared, her great breasts crammed into a red bra which was far too small for her, grinning from ear to ear.

While I was arranging my bunk one of the Russian prisoners came over.

'Are you all political?' she whispered. I nodded. 'Oh good! So am I. There were only three of us until you came. Now we must stick together against the *bladnoias.*'

'What are they?'

'Professional criminals – those women who took your things. Don't ever undress at night, or they'll have everything. My name's Vera.'

I told her mine, and then asked her why we weren't allowed into the back of the hut. Vera explained.

'That's where the bladnoia Zariza lives, the star criminal. She rules over all the other bladnoias; those who don't obey her orders are killed.'

'But what do the camp authorities say?'

'They're terrified of her themselves! They even let her have a prisoner from the men's compound in for the night when she feels like it.'

The starosta had noticed us talking and came over to separate us. Vera tried to stand up to her.

'Why shouldn't I talk to them? They're political like I am.'

The starosta didn't answer. The red bra was cutting into her flesh and impatiently she flung it off, showing her large tattooed breasts again. She hit Vera full in the face with her clenched fist, knocking her to the ground. 'Got anything else to say?'

Vera staggered to her feet. The starosta grinned. 'Next time I'll use a knife!'

The following days were taken up with medical examinations and the issue of clothing for our work in the mines. The garments we were given were immediately seized by the starosta, and any that were in good condition were exchanged for worn-out things. We were too cowed to object – with the exception of Frau Klenze from Weimar, a small, brisk woman who used to run a dress shop, who felt that something ought to be done. Secretly, in her few halting words of Russian, she complained to a guard.

Nothing was heard from the camp authorities about the complaint, at least, not that day.

'Tomorrow,' Frau Klenze said, 'something is bound to happen. It'll have to go through channels first, I suppose.'

In the morning we found her hanged in the lavatory. They had cut her breasts off, and her slashed face was unrecognizable. The girl who saw her first had a screaming fit and everyone rushed up, stopped dead at what they saw, and started to scream too. Then the starosta appeared on the scene.

'What are you all hollering about? Shut up! She's hanged herself, you can see that.' She grinned. 'That's nothing special here.'

Vera lost control of herself and lashed out at the starosta. It was the signal for battle – the thirty-eight German women and the three Russian political prisoners, against the seventy bladnoias. There would have been a massacre if the camp commandant hadn't arrived at that moment. He watched from the doorway while his guards set about us with rifle butts and quickly restored order. Anyone who resisted was bound hand and foot and lined up facing the wall. The commandant took a drag on his cigarette.

'What's been going on here?'

Vera pushed herself to the front. 'Go and look in the loo, comrade Commandant! You can see for yourself what's happened!'

He strode through the hut to the lavatory door and glanced inside.

'You see?' Vera shouted after him. 'If you don't do something, the bladnoias will kill us all!'

The commandant did see and he acted decisively. The three Russian politicals and all the Germans were moved at once to hut 11, which was empty and clean. We all heaved a sigh of relief. At last we were among ourselves and we didn't mind the three Russian women – political prisoners always stuck together in all the camps of the world.

Everyone was questioned about Frau Klenze's death and we heard later that the culprit had been found and sent to work in the brickworks.

'They call that punishment?' Brigitte was outraged. 'I

thought murderers were executed or sent to the penitentiary for the rest of their lives!'

'But this *is* the penitentiary, love,' Vera said with a bitter smile. 'All the bladnoias have life sentences anyway, so what more can they give them? Only political offenders are sentenced to death.'

'So now we know where we are,' Frau Bolevski said, 'in a penitentiary with professional criminals – and for this I fought against the Nazis for years!'

Frau Bolevski from Leipzig had been a communist since her early youth. She had been a teacher until the Nazis sacked her, but even during the dark years of the Third Reich her convictions had not wavered. After the Russian victory she had come forward eagerly to help in the formation of a truly socialist state; but her theories of communism did not agree in any way with those of the comrades from Moscow. So they got rid of her too, and she was sentenced to fifteen years' hard labour on the basis of Stalin's paragraph 56. But even in the Siberian camp she went on campaigning for the teachings of Marx and Lenin with the fervour of a prophet, and we all respected her for her integrity. Unanimously, she was elected starosta of our new barrack room.

CHAPTER FOUR

Perils of an Apprentice Pharmacist

The camp where most of the inmates of hut 11 would perish lay a few miles to the east of the city of Novosibirsk; some 2,000 men and 600 women lived behind its electrified fences. The stronger prisoners worked in the mines, the weaker ones in the woodcutter gangs, while the invalids did domestic work within the camp compound. The average winter temperature was around forty degrees of frost; but at least in the mines and in the huts it was warm.

The year was 1946, the Soviet Union was starving, and Stalin was ruling with an iron fist, just as he had done before Hitler's invasion. It was a grim time for everyone. Brigitte Muller and I worked together in the mine at a depth of 300 metres. We had to load a truck with coal and push it through a low tunnel to the conveyor belt. This was classed as 'medium grade' work, but the truck was far too heavy for us and we never managed to achieve the norm required for a bread ration – so we were always hungry. The shift ran from six in the morning to six in the evening, with half an hour for lunch and two rest breaks of a quarter of an hour each. We usually finished the food we had brought with us in the first of these, and then there would be another ten hours to go before the thin evening soup. It was a vicious circle: we became weaker every day, our output lower, and our food correspondingly less.

We were saved from collapse by Brigadier Kassim Chan, a Tartar from Kazakhstan. His appearance was a little frightening, and with his broken Russian he seemed very alien, but his heart was as soft as butter.

'You girls,' he said one day after watching our struggles, 'you need resting, you delicate, you weak. You eating!' And he gave us a piece of bread as big as a whole day's ration. Would he have done it, we wondered, if we had been old and plain? For over a week he helped us out with gifts of bread and extra rest breaks, but he too had to achieve his norm and one morning he told us:

'You girls no good for work in mine, you girls useless! You go home!'

We could hardly believe he was serious; but in fact our whole group was sent to the surface, having been reduced by four in the meantime – one dead, and three in the sick block with tuberculosis. Kassim notified the camp authorities, and from then on we worked outside with the woodcutters' brigade. That was men's work too, but it was healthier out in the open air than deep in the mine surrounded by coal dust, and the bread ration was better. Our job was to pull the huge oak trees down with ropes after the men had sawn their trunks almost through. We were supposed to jump aside quickly when a tree started to fall, but women were frequently injured by the branches. My hospital experience came in useful at last and I was able to give first aid. Kassim, who was still our supervisor, nicknamed me 'the doctor'.

In spite of the danger and hardship, I was moved by the beauty of that great Siberian forest, and could not help singing as I worked. This eccentricity eventually came to the notice of the camp commandant and I was ordered to go and sing to him! It was a very different matter singing because I was told to, in his stuffy office, in front of our gaoler, his aide, a sergeant, and the camp doctor. I managed a sentimental Ukrainian song, which they seemed to enjoy, and I even found time to notice how extraordinarily attractive the doctor was. The commandant had evidently heard about my first aid work too, as he and the doctor then agreed that I should be transferred to the sick block.

When I reported there, however, a fat and coarse-featured woman asked curtly, 'Are you a doctor?'

'Well, no, but . . .'

'In that case I have no use for you.'

'But the comrade commandant . . . '

'I can't use you and the commandant won't be able to do a thing about it!' The woman doctor waved dismissal.

After that I was sent to work in the kitchen. This was a much sought-after job and some of the women were spiteful about it. It's true that the head cook sometimes stroked my hair – but in return I was allowed to smuggle out fat, flour, sugar and vegetables. Night after night we cooked in hut 11 on the iron stove. The guards didn't notice anything, but the bladnoias did. They demanded half of the stolen food and, when this was refused, we were caught and I was back in the woodcutters' gang.

In the spring one of my friends was killed by a falling tree. Little fuss was made about dead prisoners. Their clothes were salvaged and their bodies taken to the morgue hut by the fence to wait until there was a lorry load, which never took very long. Roswitha Vocke, the art student from Berlin, had been a favourite with everyone and we couldn't bear to think of her being thrown naked into a mass grave. Frau Bolevski donated her nightdress as a shroud and Brigitte and I dressed her in it. As a precaution we went to the morgue hut again the next night, and sure enough the nightdress had been stolen. So the women of hut 11 sewed a shroud from paper and attached a few coloured bits of rag to it; on the third night we dressed Roswitha again. Next day as we were returning from work we met the lorry taking the bodies away. It was windy, and the newspapers which normally covered them had blown off. Roswitha lay on top wearing the paper shroud, and the coloured rags glowed like funeral flowers.

Suddenly Brigitte began to pray: 'Our Father . . . ' We all joined in and the guards waited for us to finish.

Towards the end of that summer I got caught by a large oak branch which broke my left leg and found myself back in the sick block as a patient. The fat woman doctor, comrade Varvara Komorova, put the leg in plaster without setting it first and I lay all night in great pain, worrying about being permanently crippled. Early in the morning I called the nurse and demanded a pair of scissors. She was a simple, good-natured soul, a prisoner from Alma Ata, and she watched open-mouthed as I cut open the plaster and splinted my leg with a plank from my wooden bunk.

'How is possible?' she asked in her broken Russian. 'You doctor?'

'Something like that.' I didn't feel like explaining. 'Now I need some more plaster. Go and get the doctor, will you?'

The fat comrade would be furious, but I didn't care; my leg was more important.

It wasn't Dr Komorova who came to see me, but the handsome major I had met in the commandant's office.

'Aha, it's our nightingale,' he exclaimed cheerfully, and he bent over my leg. 'Good heavens, you've done that very well indeed! Such talent is wasted on the trees; you'd be much more useful here.'

I was quite bowled over by his friendliness, and also, it must be admitted, by his beautiful dark eyes and soft hair. For the first time since Andrei had gone, almost a year ago, I felt the stirrings of interest in a man.

He took me to the hospital in Novosibirsk for an X-ray, and there my leg was properly splinted and plastered. Back in the camp sick block, I saw him every other day, for Dr Komorova and he were on duty alternately. He never passed my bed without a smile and a kind word, and I soon began to love him with a shy devotion, as a being from another world of light, warmth and hope.

When my leg had healed Dr Stremilov arranged for me to stay on in the laboratory as a pharmacist. This gave me some importance among the prisoners; it quickly became known, not only that I spoke Russian, but also that I could make up medicines and pills for a lot of the more common ailments.

Needless to say the bladnoias heard about it too, although their hut was now segregated from the rest of the camp by an extra barbed wire fence. One evening as I was leaving the sick block two women barred my way.

'Come with us, we need you!' It was the rough voice of the starosta from hut 17. I hesitated, wondering whether to shout for help; but the starosta had a knife in her hand.

'This'll be in your belly if you make a sound. Come on!'

I crawled with them through a hole in the wire. Hut 17 was just as I remembered it, over-heated, ill-lit and smelly. This time, however, I was taken through to the forbidden quarters at the back. We stopped in front of a curtained alcove.

'The German girl is here,' the starosta announced.

'Okay, you can open up.'

I recognized that clear, slightly sharp voice, and when the starosta had drawn back the curtains with something like the flourish of a master of ceremonies, I saw the bladnoia Zariza for the first time. She was young, blonde, naked except for black silk briefs, lying on a bed with white sheets and an embroidered pillowcase. There was a white sheepskin rug on the floor, a vodka bottle and glasses on the bedside table. A selection of dresses and nightgowns hung on the wall above her, and beside her pillow lay a knife.

'Come here, German!'

My knees were shaking as I obeyed.

'Are you afraid of me?' I swallowed dumbly.

'You know who I am, of course?'

Without thinking, I dropped a curtsey and kissed her outstretched hand. The Zariza laughed.

'I can see you come from a good family, just like me.' She raised herself on her elbows, took the vodka bottle and filled a glass. Her pale skin was covered with scars. I was staring, fascinated, at one which ran diagonally across her right breast, when she spoke again.

'These aren't war wounds, you know, but they're just as hard-earned; you don't become a leader for nothing.' She handed me the glass.

'You needn't be afraid of me, German. Just help me and I'll help you.'

The vodka was giving me courage. As soon as my glass was empty the Zariza filled it again. Then she asked,

'Are you a doctor?'

'No, I'm not.'

'But you are a pharmacist?'

'No, not that either.'

'Well, it doesn't make any odds really. I've no choice and you do know something about medicine, so they tell me.'

'What do you want me to do?'

The Zariza lay back on her pillows. 'I am pregnant and you must abort the baby.'

I knew very little about pregnancy and childbirth and even less about abortions. There was nothing I could do for her, and my heart sank.

'Why don't you have it?' I blurted out. 'After all, you could afford to . . . ' I waved vaguely at the luxury surrounding her. The Zariza shook her head.

'Don't be a fool, German! We'd all like to have children, believe it or not. But do you know what happens then? They leave it with you for two years, and when it starts to speak, when it learns to call you "Mummy", they take it away and put it in a state home. And you stay here and you never see your child again.' The hard young face was close to tears. 'No, I'm not going through that! You must get rid of it.'

'But I don't know what to do!'

'Of course you do. There are medicines, and you will provide them if you know what's good for you. If you let me down, you're finished, understand?' I nodded miserably.

Suddenly the Zariza was all smiles. 'That's settled, then. Come back tomorrow night and bring the stuff. You can go now.'

I didn't dare ask anyone's advice, but searched the laboratory shelves hoping for inspiration. Quinine! Surely I had heard that mentioned in connection with abortions! I mixed a large quantity in distilled water and gave the bottle to the starosta next evening. For three days nothing happened; then she came to the sick block complaining of a sore throat and insisted on seeing me privately.

'That damned stuff didn't have any effect at all,' she hissed as soon as we were alone. 'What do you think you're playing at? You'll soon be at your own funeral if you can't do any better. The Zariza is getting impatient!'

I couldn't help sobbing with despair and helplessness, though this only increased the starosta's contempt. She wouldn't listen to my protestations of ignorance. 'We'll give you until to-morrow night!' she spat at me and stormed out.

The nurse, Katya, put her head round the door. 'What on earth did she want? Don't have anything to do with that lot! What's the matter? Why are you crying?'

Katya was a woman of about fifty who had served six years of her ten-year sentence. She had a daughter of my age, to whom she was devoted. I decided that my only hope was to trust her and I told her everything. Her reaction was brisk and practical.

'Potassium permanganate, a solution of one part in ten – no stronger! And don't thank me; I want nothing to do with it.'

Next evening the starosta was again waiting at the fence. I gave her the bag of crystals and told her how to make up the solution. A few days later she hobbled into the sick block.

'My foot, it's my foot! I can hardly walk!'

With a sinking heart I helped her to a chair.

'You fucking bitch!' she whispered. 'You've poisoned the Zariza! She's on her last legs, and if you don't come and save her I'll tear your guts out!'

'What's wrong with her?'

'You'll see soon enough!'

'But I'm not a doctor, I can't . . . '

'You've got to, or you'll be strung up in the lavatory. Now, hurry!'

'Just hang on a moment.' I ran to find Katya; she was scrubbing the floor in the next room. 'Katya, the Zariza is dying!'

The older woman's face went grey. 'I told you I didn't want to have anything to do with it.'

I pleaded with her, and reluctantly she agreed to come, on condition that we never spoke of it again. She made the sign of the Cross as she got up from the floor.

In the bladnoias' hut we found the Zariza lying on her luxurious bed screaming and writhing with pain. Her women were fussing about trying to comfort her, but to no avail.

'Get out of the way!' the starosta shouted, 'the German is here.' She took a knife from her pocket and pushed us forward. 'Now then, do something!'

The abortion had been successful – even I could see that – but the placenta had not come away, and there were burns from the potassium permanganate on the Zariza's thighs. Probably they had made the solution too strong, in spite of my warnings. Katya sized up the situation at a glance, called for hot water and clean cloths, and told two of the women to hold the patient down. Then she set to work, without instruments, without anaesthetics, while the rest of us watched, awestruck.

An hour later, Katya straightened herself and wiped the

sweat from her broad peasant face. 'Let her sleep now.'

The Zariza was lying still and quiet, and deathly pale.

'Will she be all right?' The starosta's voice was full of suspicion.

'Of course she will!' Katya snapped. 'Now take us back!'

The starosta escorted us to the hole in the fence. 'If she dies, I'll kill you!' she muttered to me as Katya was climbing through, and I had no doubt at all that she meant it.

CHAPTER FIVE

The Blizzard

A strange week followed. I was sick with fear that the Zariza might die, and each evening as darkness fell I half expected the starosta to step out of the shadows with her knife. I longed to confide in someone, or even to talk to Katya, but she went stolidly about her work, avoiding my eye, and I dared not break my promise.

At the same time, I couldn't help noticing that Dr Stremilov was coming more and more often to the laboratory. There wasn't much for him to do there, but he would talk to me, ask me about my past, even occasionally stroke my hair. If the idea hadn't been so preposterous, I might have imagined that he was fond of me. My terror alternated with a tremulous excitement.

At dusk on the eighth day, as I was leaving the sick block, the starosta barred my way as I had expected. I was too frightened even to scream. She grabbed my arm.

'The Zariza sends her regards. She is okay again, and she says, if you are ever in any trouble, you are to come to her.'

That was the last I saw of any of the bladnoias. My only enemy now was that fat Dr Komorova, who tried to make my life difficult in little ways – because, according to Dr Stremilov, she didn't like pretty girls. But I was soon past caring. Stremilov had caught me singing in the laboratory one day and had kissed me and declared his love. Starved of affection as I was, I would have fallen for anyone; it seemed miraculous to be chosen by a man who had already been my hero for months.

More miracles were to follow. Juri – who was a close friend of the commandant's – managed to get passes for me to leave the camp on pretext of collecting medicines from the pharmacy in Novosibirsk. Then we would go to his flat, where he provided clothes for me to change into, and we would light up the samovar and have tea and pretend for an hour or so that we were an ordinary courting couple. Once, he even took me out dancing; it was so unbelievably wonderful that I never noticed how late it was until the music stopped. I was horrified, but Juri seemed unconcerned.

'Whatever will the guard say?' I asked him.

'He won't say anything at all. You have been on night duty at the general hospital.'

'But will he believe that?'

'If I tell him so, he'll believe it. He's a patient of mine; I treated him with a bottle of vodka only this afternoon.' He kissed me. 'Did you enjoy your outing?'

'Oh, Juri! And yet – it's dangerous, too. Suppose somebody asks my name!'

'That's all right. Your name is Jelena . . . What is your father's name?'

'Karl.'

'So you are Jelena Kirilovna from Leningrad – no, Lemburg. Now we only need a surname. Let's see – how about Pushkova? That sounds fine, doesn't it?'

'Jelena Kirilovna Pushkova,' I repeated – with no idea that I should be stuck with that name for the next eight years.

It was four o'clock in the morning when we got back to the camp, yet no one said anything. A guard escorted me to hut 11; I tiptoed past the rows of grey-faced sleeping women and climbed into my bunk. Below me, Brigitte was awake.

'Wherever have you been?' she whispered.

'I was on duty . . . at the hospital.' It didn't sound very convincing. Brigitte giggled. I lay in the dark longing to confide in her, and finally I climbed down and got into her bunk.

'Swear that you won't tell anybody . . . '

*

As autumn deepened into winter, there were many deaths in our hut. Western Europeans could not adapt to Siberian conditions, and one by one the older women succumbed to tuber-culosis, malnutrition or heart disease. My secret happiness gave me strength, but it also gave me a sense of obligation towards the others. I stole from the sick block everything I could lay my hands on that might give them some comfort. Juri made sure of the supplies, not without risk to himself; but, as I had already learnt, his was a character that thrived on taking chances.

Gauze and cottonwool were particularly useful. The women sandwiched them together and stitched them into quilts and curtains, or, dyed pale blue with diluted ink, into dresses and jackets. On one of his rounds the commandant even compli-mented us on the cosy appearance of the hut. He must have known where the materials came from, but Juri was his friend and he said nothing.

However, the bonanza couldn't last. One evening an elderly prisoner had a heart attack and unfortunately Dr Komorova was on duty. The woman was dead by the time she arrived; but she noticed the quilted blanket with which we had covered her and quickly realized what it was made of.

'Only you could have stolen that!' she raged at me. 'This is the last straw! Just you wait till I've finished with you!' She stormed out, leaving me once again weak-kneed with fear.

Next morning I was called to the commandant's office. I was no longer in awe of him and readily admitted my guilt.

'But it did look very nice, comrade Commandant. You said so yourself, remember? You said our hut was the nicest in the whole camp.'

'That's quite true,' he laughed, 'but Dr Komorova is furious with you. She won't have you in the laboratory any more and there's nothing I can do about it. I should really put you in the arrest block; however, I think we can dispense with that. The question is, what are we to do with you?'

I held my breath and waited while he shuffled the papers on his desk.

'Here we are,' he said at last. 'They need two cleaning women over at the Cultural Centre. Report there tomorrow morning. And take a friend.'

*

Never had the Cultural Centre been more enthusiastically cleaned. Brigitte and I washed the curtains, scrubbed the floors and polished everything until the place was hardly recognizable. In some ways it was an even better job than working in the laboratory; no one supervised us, and as it was outside the camp there was no prison atmosphere. The Centre was used as a social club by the free miners who lived locally; they were friendly and sympathetic and made sure that we had plenty to eat.

When they discovered that Brigitte could play the piano and I could sing, we were asked to perform at their annual party, 7 November, the anniversary of the Bolshevik Revolution. Everyone came – the commandant, the Party secretary, the two camp doctors. We went through our whole repertoire of German and Russian songs, to thunderous applause, and were 'paid' with a huge basket of *piroshki* – a sort of doughnut filled with meat, cabbage and onions.

The women in hut 11 could hardly believe their eyes. Frau Bolevski gave us one of her rare smiles and, as a good communist, she saw to it that the piroshki were shared out equally. As a good starosta, she also had to ensure that no one ate too much too quickly, as the food was a bit rich for starving stomachs. For once, the whole hut was comfortably replete when we settled down for the night.

At one o'clock in the morning there was a hammering on the door.

'The two singers out!'

Our hearts sank. But it was only Juri and the commandant – who insisted that we called him Kostya – both rather the worse for drink. We were whisked off into Novosibirsk, where Kostya also had a flat, and didn't meet again until the morning when we had to clean up the Cultural Centre after the festivities.

It proved to have been one indiscretion too many. Dr Komorova discovered that we had been out all night, and with whom, and she threatened to make trouble for our benefactors. Brigitte and I lost our pleasant cleaning job and were put on to yard duty at the camp. This consisted of cutting firewood, moving dustbins and carrying water from the pump to the huts. And snow-sweeping; every morning the parade ground had to be clear of snow for the daily roll-call.

Juri had warned me that we wouldn't be able to meet for a while, but he had promised to try and arrange something at Christmas. Late on Christmas Eve there was still no word from him. When the other women came in from work they noticed that I had done my hair and started teasing me.

'There are no Christmas parties here, you know!'

'Oh, come on,' Brigitte said, 'why should we listen to this? We might as well go out and clear the snow ready for to-morrow. Anything's better than staying cooped up in the hut.'

Vera, the Russian political, was drying her wet foot rags over the stove.

'I wouldn't if I were you,' she said. 'There's a blizzard coming. Can't you hear the wind?'

I went to the door and looked outside. Snow was falling in thick flakes and swirling round the buildings, but in the west the evening sky looked red and harmless.

'It's all right. Let's go!'

Brigitte and I put on our heavy boots and quilted coats, collected our shovels, and trudged over to the alarm fence at the far end of the yard. From there we started working methodically back towards the hut. It crossed my mind that if Juri did come, escape would be easier if we were outside already. But there was nobody about. I felt absolutely crushed with disappointment. Brigitte began talking about her family in Dresden and how they would be spending Christmas. We both felt so pathetic and neglected that in the end we just huddled together and cried.

Suddenly a gust of icy wind knocked us over. The sky wasn't red any more, but pitch black. A solid wall of snow was pressing us back towards the electric fence; the crystals stung my face and I lay flat, trying to inch forward against it. I couldn't see Brigitte, or anything else; when I screamed the wind carried the sound away and filled my mouth with snow. After that there was only a suffocating darkness.

A long time later, I woke up. There was a red wooden ceiling above me, and I was lying on something hard and cold. With an effort, I turned my head and looked straight into a woman's face. Her skin was waxy, her eyes stared blindly into mine, and after a minute or two I realized she was dead.

There were more bodies on the other side of me; I was in the morgue hut. I shouted for help, but no one came, and I decided I must be dead myself. With a feeling almost of relief, I lost consciousness again.

Next time I woke I was in a bed, and Juri was bending over me.

'I dreamed I had died!'

'You almost did, Lenotchka.'

'Brigitte! Where is Brigitte?'

'Never mind now. I'll tell you later. First, listen to me. You're not in the camp; you're in an isolation ward at the general hospital. Nobody knows you're a prisoner, so don't speak German whatever you do. Try not to say anything unless I'm around. Do you understand?'

He waited until I found the strength to nod, and then I felt the prick of a hypodermic. I drifted off to sleep again, and each time I woke, 'Don't speak German', was the first thought I had. It was really too much trouble to speak at all; my head was full of confused dreams and I could hardly distinguish between sleep and waking.

Eventually I opened my eyes and saw the room I was in quite clearly. Juri was sitting on a chair beside the bed, wearing a white overall, with his stethoscope hanging out of the pocket. I knew I wasn't dreaming and I felt hungry. Juri fetched me a bowl of soup.

'Is Christmas over?' I asked him.

'It was over three weeks ago. You've been very ill.'

'Why didn't you come for us? You promised!'

'I only promised to try, love, and it was impossible. The Komorova never let me out of her sight.'

'How am I here, then?'

'It's quite a story, Lenotchka!'

Apparently, after the blizzard Brigitte and I had been dug out of the snow and taken to the sick block, where Dr Komorova had pronounced us both dead. As soon as Juri heard about it he had rushed to the morgue hut, realized that it might be possible to revive me and removed my 'body', saying that he needed it for dissection. He had brought me into the hospital as a suspected case of typhoid – hence the isolation ward.

'And Brigitte?' I already knew what he would say.

'There was nothing I could have done for her. She had been blown against the fence and electrocuted. I'm sorry.'

I wept for my friend. When I was calmer, Juri became brisk and cheerful again.

'You'll be all right now, my love. I've got hold of a marvellous new drug for you, called penicillin.' He glanced at his watch. 'I must go now, but I'll send the nurse in. And don't forget – no German!'

'What am I to say, then, if she asks me anything?'

He took down a slate from the end of the bed. On it was written: 'Jelena Kirilovna Pushkova, student, aged nineteen.'

'This is your real name now. The prisoner Helga Wannenmacher doesn't exist. She's dead.'

CHAPTER SIX

Enter a Female Vet

While I lay in hospital slowly recovering, Juri was busy setting me up as a Soviet citizen. He took my photograph in the X-ray department and got me an identity card from the Novosibirsk police. I was amazed that this was possible, but when I asked Juri how he did it, he laughed.

'I told them you were brought in unconscious and your clothes were burnt for fear of typhoid infection. Unfortunately your identity card was in your coat pocket, so that got burnt too.'

'And they believed you?'

'Why should they doubt the word of a doctor, a major in the glorious Soviet Army?'

He came to see me every day; no longer a demi-god condescending to one of the unfortunates in his care, but a fellow-conspirator and equal, full of eager plans. Only once did I see him annoyed, when I asked how things were at the camp.

'Jelena Pushkova, you don't know anything about labour camps; you've never seen one. Don't speak of it again!'

I was discharged from the hospital in mid-March and spent a few weeks' convalescence as a guest of one of Juri's patients, Anya Fyodorova. Juri provided me with the sort of clothes that young Russian women wore and I was passed off as Anya's niece, who was a student in Moscow. It all seemed so easy and at last I began to relax – though I hardly left the house.

Then, one spring morning, Juri and I together got on the

49

Trans-Siberian Express, bound for Moscow ourselves, where his sister had a flat. The journey took four days and it could hardly have been more different from the nightmare weeks of going east in the convict train. We travelled first class, had meals in the dining car and were surrounded by comfort and attention. I was as excited as a child, though slightly apprehensive about meeting Juri's sister, who was a lecturer in history at the university.

'You needn't be frightened of Sonya,' he kept telling me. 'We get on very well. I've told her you're coming and I'm sure you'll be friends in no time.'

Sonya met us at the station and we took the Underground to her flat. It consisted of two rooms, one for her and one for Juri, with cooking arrangements on the landing. I was bewildered, and still overwhelmed by the splendours of the Moscow Underground, and sat speechless while Juri told his sister my adventures. Then he said that I would need a work permit.

'Oh!' Sonya was obviously taken aback. 'You want to get married?'

'Of course we do,' Juri beamed. 'Otherwise she can't stay in Moscow.'

'No, she can't, can she?' Sonya looked very steadily at her brother. 'Well, I'll make some tea.' She picked up the samovar.

'I'll give you a hand,' said Juri and followed her outside.

I was left sitting on the sofa and feeling very depressed. Obviously, Sonya didn't approve of me. But when they came back into the room she was quite friendly and immediately launched into the all-important question of what to wear for the wedding.

*

I got married in a white woollen suit which was secondhand, but looked like new, for which Juri had paid eighty roubles. His wedding present was a gold necklace with a ruby pendant. Dressed for the ceremony, I felt, for the first time, utterly unlike a prisoner. But Sonya could see that my problems were not really over.

'Jelena speaks excellent Russian, but that is just about all,' she said over tea next day. 'What does she know about life in the Soviet Union, or about Russian history, art and literature?

It will seem odd for an officer's wife to be so ignorant!'

After some discussion, she and Juri decided that I should enrol at the university. To do that, I had to be transferred from a provincial university, and, since Lemburg was the birthplace on my identity card, it seemed the obvious choice. So Juri and I went to Lemburg for a sort of honeymoon. It was a starving city and there was a black market in everything, including documents. It took Juri eight days and 20,000 roubles to obtain a valid transfer for Jelena Kirilovna Pushkova from Lemburg to Moscow university.

We had another week in Moscow, seeing the sights, and then Juri's leave was up. Sonya and I saw him off on the train back to Novosibirsk, and soon afterwards I started work. I had chosen a course in engineering science – geology, chemistry and mechanics – and for the first day or two I couldn't understand a word of the lectures. I would go home to Sonya in despair, but she encouraged me, and assured me I would soon get the hang of it. Then I began to make friends among my fellow-students and they helped me too. Like them, I joined Komsomol, the Organization of Young Communists, and swore on oath to become not only a good communist but also a good engineer.

Towards the end of term I felt confident enough to write to my parents in Güsten – in Russian, of course. I told them that I was well, that I was studying at Moscow University and that I had got married, and signed myself Jelena Pushkova. Three weeks later I had a reply from my mother, also in Russian. Her letter was as discreet as mine, simply saying they were delighted to hear from me and hoped I would visit them when I had finished my course. That hardly seemed likely, but at least they knew I was alive.

Juri came on leave again in the autumn and we had a few wonderful weeks together. He had applied for a transfer to Moscow and was confident that it would be through by the spring, so I saw him off on the Trans-Siberian Express, cheerfully thinking that it was for the last time.

Soon after my second term started, Sonya had to go to Kiev for a few days to attend a congress. I was alone in the flat, cooking my supper on the little stove on the landing, when a tall, thickset woman came stumping up the stairs. She wore a

51

major's uniform with the insignia of a veterinary surgeon, and she was carrying a large suitcase. Without a word, she pushed past me and went to Juri's room. Finding it empty, she came back.

'Would you by any chance know where my husband is?'

I smiled at her. 'Perhaps if you could tell me his name?'

The stranger snorted impatiently. 'Dr Stremilov, of course!'

I felt my knees giving way, but somehow I managed to answer her. 'Dr Stremilov is not here. He works in Novosibirsk.'

'Well, what about Sonya, his sister?'

'She's not here either at the moment.'

'I see,' the woman said, looking me over. 'And what are you doing here, if I may ask?'

I blurted out something about being a student to whom Sonya had offered accommodation.

'And why is my husband's room unlocked?'

'I've just finished cleaning it. Sonya asked me to.'

The woman suddenly became quite amiable. 'Well, that's all right then. I can move in straight away.'

Our wedding photograph was on the bedside table and I just had time to snatch it up before Juri's wife followed me into the room and heaved her suitcase on to the bed.

'It's good to be back in Moscow,' she remarked, wiping her forehead with an enormous handkerchief. 'I am sweating like a pig. I'll go and have a bath, and then we'll have tea together. All right?' She seemed to be in the habit of giving orders.

As soon as she was safely in the bathroom I rushed downstairs to the public telephone and rang my friend Vyka at the university.

'Pack your bags and come over,' Vyka said. 'Sonya will sort it out when she gets back.'

I dashed back upstairs, scribbled a note to tell Sonya where I was, packed my things and was out of the house before the woman returned from her bath. I still couldn't believe that Juri had deceived me, but I was too frightened to stay and argue. All I wanted to do was to get away.

*

Two or three days later, Sonya telephoned. 'I've just got home.

I have to come and talk to you about Nina.'

'Who is Nina?'

'You know. Where can I meet you?'

'Is she Juri's wife?'

'Not on the telephone, Jelena. Can I come and see you straight away?'

I couldn't wait. 'Sonya, just tell me, is she married to Juri or not?'

There was a little silence at the other end; then Sonya's reluctant voice. 'Well, yes, she is – but only on paper!'

'Thank you!' I said, and hung up quickly so that she wouldn't hear my sobs. When the storm of weeping had subsided, I sat down and wrote Juri a letter – the sort of letter one writes when one is twenty and has just been cruelly betrayed. I told him, among other things, that I never wanted to see him again.

I went straight out and posted it as soon as it was finished, and when I came back, Sonya was waiting in my room.

'You must let me explain, Jelena!'

'What is there to explain? You knew all along that he was already married!'

'Yes, but he asked me not to tell you. Poor Juri! It was wrong of him, I suppose, but his life's in such a muddle.'

Sonya went on to tell me about her brother's marriage. It had been a hasty war wedding, in 1939, on the Finnish front where they had been serving as doctor and vet. Nina had pretended to be pregnant, and when Juri found he had been tricked, they had quarrelled and parted. Nina had kept her marriage lines, but by some oversight the event had never been recorded in Juri's papers. If he applied for a divorce, he would be in trouble and she had no intention of divorcing him.

By the end of the story I was crying as much for Juri as for myself.

'Why has she come back?' I sobbed. 'What does she want?'

Sonya sighed. 'She's fed up with living in a peasant commune. She wants to live in Moscow as Juri's wife.'

*

A week later I had an answer to my letter. 'Stay where you are. I'll come as soon as I can. Everything will be all right!'

But it wasn't. Sonya let me know when Juri was coming and

I went to the station to meet him. Nina was already there. I hid behind a pillar and watched them greet each other warmly and hurry away arm in arm. Then I waited in my room for three days, and by the time Juri did at last turn up, I was too hurt and angry to let him kiss me.

'How could you leave me alone so long! Where have you been? Not with Nina!'

'But Lenotchka, she is my wife, after all!'

'And what am I?'

'You are the one I love,' he said, and gave me his old irresistible smile. 'Listen, sweetheart, the most important thing now is to get the marriage deleted from the register.'

I didn't grasp it at once. Then my knees started giving way and I whimpered, 'Which marriage?'

'Well, ours, of course. Then I shall try to get a divorce from Nina.'

'What do you mean, you'll try?'

'I'm not at all sure that she'll agree. She doesn't have to.'

'And what if she refuses?'

'Then you and I will have to live in sin, my love, won't we?'

He flashed me that smile again, but somehow the magic had gone out of it and I suddenly realized why.

'Juri, I do believe you're afraid of her!'

'No, no, of course not! But I must consider her feelings.'

And who is going to consider my feelings, I wondered. They were surprisingly calm, as it happened, and I told Juri I wouldn't see him again until the situation was sorted out. If I had expected a protest, I was disappointed.

'That's very sensible of you, Lenotchka. I hope you can go on staying here; and don't worry. When things are settled I'll get in touch with you.'

As I opened the door for him, something snapped.

'Don't bother!' I said, and this time I really meant it. I wouldn't accept his money; I returned his letters unopened. Then one day Sonya came to see me. She told me that, as a result of a substantial bribe, our marriage had been annulled; also that Nina was still in the flat and showed no inclination to leave.

'I am so sorry, Jelena. Believe me, it hasn't been easy for Juri either!'

When she had gone, I broke down. It was partly the thought of Juri and Nina sharing that room where he and I had been so happy; partly the bitter discovery that truth could be altered, a marriage obliterated, if the price was right. Life seemed pointless – but what was the best way of ending it? In films and novels there was never any problem, but I had no revolver, no pills.

In the end I bought a litre of ink and drank the lot. It made me very ill, but I didn't die. When Sonya realized how desperate I was, she helped me in every possible way. Not only did she talk me out of my despair; she also managed to get me a government grant of 800 roubles a month so that I could continue my course at the university independently of Juri. I was duly grateful for all this, and I worked hard, attended the incredibly boring meetings of the Young Communists' club, and did my best to become a model student.

Perhaps one day I might have become a good engineer; it was never put to the test. Vyka and I were working one evening in the room we shared, when there was a knock on the door.

'I'll see who that is,' she said, and went to open it. I could hardly believe what happened next.

'I am sorry to disturb you,' said a voice from the past. 'I am looking for a student called Jelena Kirilovna Pushkova; they said I would find her here. My name is Andrei Sidrov.'

CHAPTER SEVEN

Night in the Mountains

We went to a restaurant and talked for hours over a bottle of wine. There was so much explaining to do! Andrei was now a full colonel, on a staff course at the Moscow Military Academy; he had kept in touch with a friend in Güsten who had told him of my arrest and sentence. Just recently, this friend had written again telling him about the letter I'd sent to my mother – and Andrei had all the information he needed to track me down.

He listened incredulously to my adventures, and I was a little hurt to learn later that he had carefully checked everything I'd told him. He went to see Sonya Stremilova and satisfied himself that my marriage had really been annulled; he made sure that Jelena Kirilovna Pushkova was properly registered with the police; and he enquired about my record with the Komsomol. As he pointed out, an officer at the Academy couldn't afford the slightest irregularity – in himself or in his wife. Then, for the second time, he asked me to marry him.

We went to Gorki for the wedding, where his parents lived. The festivities went on for three days, and by far the liveliest guest was General Shemyakin, Andrei's CO. He was a great character, and I took to him at once. One of his best stories – which he told a good many times in the course of the celebrations – was of how he, personally, had hoisted the Red Flag on top of the Reichstag after the fall of Berlin, and all the credit had gone to one of his sergeants. But secretly, so Andrei

56

assured me, the general had a tremendous admiration for the West. We told him the truth about my background and he wasn't in the least shocked.

So I was delighted when General Shemyakin was appointed to the command of a missile research station in the Caucasus and asked for Andrei as his deputy. We moved to Kirovabad, where we had a large house, with servants, and a garden where lemon and orange trees grew. It was an idyllic life; we travelled, entertained, went hunting in the mountains, spent week-ends by the Caspian Sea.

I wasn't used to so much leisure, and after a time I got permission to work at the research station as an interpreter. At the end of the war, a great many German scientists and engineers had been drafted to the Soviet Union and Kirovabad had its complement. I invited two of them to spend Christmas with us and laid on a real German feast, with candles and decorations and presents round the tree. Herr Wilpert and Herr Osten were quite overcome with gratitude and homesickness, and expressed their amazement that a Russian woman could have got all the details right. If only they'd known, the occasion was just as nostalgic for me as it was for them!

We had a year of almost perfect happiness, culminating, in the spring of 1949, with the discovery that I was pregnant. Andrei was so excited that he insisted on telling everybody; and I, too, was more pleased than I would have thought possible. It really began to look as if my misfortunes were over; indeed, life seemed almost too good to be true.

It was. That summer I had a worried letter from Sonya. Juri had been discharged from the army and couldn't get a job. She gave no details, except that it was 'all Nina's fault', and she ended by asking whether, in my newly-influential position, I could do anything to help him. Well, he had saved my life once, and I could hardly refuse. I showed the letter to Andrei and he spoke to General Shemyakin, who admitted that the research station could do with another doctor. Juri was to come for an interview.

He arrived, unannounced, one hot July afternoon while Andrei was still at the office. We had tea together on the terrace overlooking the garden. At first, Juri seemed in the highest spirits, teasing me about the baby and saying how lucky it was he'd come just when I needed a good doctor. Then he fell silent, looked around him thoughtfully, and said:

'It's nice here. Perhaps the KGB would leave me alone.'

'Juri! What *do* you mean?' Those three letters terrified me, as they did anyone in Russia at that time, and their shadow fell across the day.

Then he launched into a long story. I had always believed what he said – I couldn't help it – and to this day I don't know how much of it was true. The gist of it was that Nina had gone to Novosibirsk to try and find out why Juri wanted a divorce. She had made friends with Dr Komorova and learnt a lot, but had not made any fuss until after the divorce had been granted. Then she had denounced Juri for having an affair with a German prisoner, and for misuse of valuable medicines and materials at the labour camp. Nothing could be proved, as the women's section had since been closed down, but they had sacked him anyway.

'They may have been glad of an excuse,' Juri grinned sheepishly. 'I did drink a bit, as you know, and I've never been mad on rules and regulations.'

I couldn't help smiling at those two understatements. But nothing so far explained why the KGB was interested in him.

'Then,' Juri continued, 'I was summoned to Moscow for questioning. Someone at central office had got the idea that Helga Wannenmacher and Jelena Pushkova might be one and the same person.'

'*No!*' The fears that I had almost banished came crowding back and I saw my life with Andrei as the charade it was. The poised and confident colonel's wife was still a fugitive after all. I hardly heard Juri as he hurried on.

'Of course I told them that the prisoner Wannenmacher's death had been certified and her file closed. And that Jelena Pushkova was a Ukrainian from Lemburg – no connection at all. They seemed satisfied; but last week they sent for me again. I don't know what they really think.'

His eyes restlessly avoided mine. 'Would you have a small vodka for an old friend?'

*

Juri settled down as a guest in our house and made himself

charming to everybody. But he didn't seem at all anxious to start work. General Shemyakin offered him a job at the research station and to Andrei's dismay he turned it down. I could understand that; it meant a security screening in Moscow. But I couldn't understand it when he refused a job at the municipal hospital, which was desperate for more doctors.

He always had money to spend, too, which puzzled me until one day I found a suitcase full of cigarettes in his room, and he made no bones about the fact that he was selling them in the bazaar. Andrei was scandalized.

'You know I like him, darling, but I simply cannot have a black marketeer in my house. Surely he must understand that.'

So Juri took a room in the town and continued on his downward path. General Shemyakin retired and Andrei became acting commander of the station. If the appointment was confirmed, he would himself be promoted to general; but before that happened he was suddenly summoned to Moscow. He came back looking worried. The KGB had reopened the Güsten affair

*

I could feel the net tightening. Andrei tried to reassure me that, in his position, he would be able to protect me and no one would doubt his word. But Juri played upon my fears and added new ones. Andrei's career would be ruined, he said, when the truth came out, and this upset me more than the thought of going back to prison.

'We must go away, Lenotchka,' Juri said. 'It's the only thing to do; we're both in dead trouble. Luckily it's easy from here. The Persian border is only a hundred miles away. We've just got to go through the mountains and over the River Araks.'

'Don't forget I'm six months pregnant! And anyway, I wouldn't dream of leaving Andrei.'

Nothing more was said, but once the idea of escape had been planted, I couldn't get it out of my mind.

Then a commission from Moscow came to inspect the base. In my overwrought state, I felt sure they had come to inspect me and I pleaded with Andrei to take me to Persia. He stared at me as though I had suggested a trip to the moon.

'Leave Russia – are you mad? Go over to the capitalists? How could you suggest such a thing?'

But at the end of September he was called to Moscow again and he wouldn't tell me why.

'Now is the time!' Juri said as soon as Andrei had gone. 'I've got it all worked out. Your German friends, Wilpert and Osten, are coming too; they've been wanting to escape for ages. I've found a chap with a van who'll take us to the mountains; then we'll walk, and somebody else will get us over the river.'

'Who are these people?'

'Oh,' he replied airily, 'they're smugglers I met in the bazaar, very trustworthy. We pay them with firearms. Are you coming? We start in three days' time, but I must have your answer now.'

I must really have been mad; I said yes.

'Good girl!' Juri grinned. 'Give me a pistol, then.'

I gave him Andrei's Mauser. Two days later he was back with final instructions.

'Be at the Central Station tomorrow evening at six. A van from the commune will be standing there; the driver has been paid already. Don't forget to bring food for six days. Have you got a small vodka for an old friend?' He drank it like water. 'Oh yes, I almost forgot – I need another two hunting rifles.'

I gave him two of Andrei's. Next day I packed a suitcase and got our chauffeur to drive me to the station, having let it be known that I was going to join my husband in Moscow. I left a note for Andrei which I hoped would exonerate him simply saying that I was running away with Juri because I loved him. It took me several attempts to get it right.

The van was there and the men were equipped as if for a hunting trip, which was perfectly normal in Kirovabad. We drove some twenty miles into the mountains; then the van put us down and turned back, and we set up our little tent and camped for the night. Juri had come up beforehand and cached the pistols which were to pay our guides – and we spent the whole of the next day looking for them. He simply couldn't remember where they were; and when I accused him of having been drunk when he hid them, he just nodded grimly. We found them too late in the evening to make a start and had to spend another night in the same place. It wasn't a very good beginning.

All next day we walked southwards, and in the evening we came to the home of one of the smugglers. He appeared to be doing very nicely; he had a large, comfortable house and several wives. Juri handed over some of the pistols in exchange for a room for the night and instructions for the next stage.

It was a three-day march from there to a shepherd's hut, over much more difficult ground. I soon realized that I wasn't going to make it and begged Juri to let me go back. He wouldn't hear of it; instead he improvized a litter and the men took turns to carry me.

We found the hut all right, but the shepherd wasn't there. Juri and the two Germans each set off in a different direction to look for him, leaving me alone. It wasn't long before I discovered that the hut was crawling with snakes. Shuddering, I climbed on to a bench and crouched there, trying to keep an eye on them all, and listening to the jackals howling in the woods outside. By the time the men returned I was quite rigid with terror.

The shepherd threw buckets of water over the snakes and shooed them away as if they were bothersome chickens. He was a wild-looking character, but he spoke a little Russian, and I decided I would have to appeal to him to get me out of this adventure. When the others were asleep, I tackled him.

'Could you take me back to Kirovabad?'

He shook his head decisively. Probably he had a sound reason for keeping away from civilization, but I was pretty desperate. I patted my belly and made signs to show that I was utterly exhausted. At last he nodded.

'I have donkey. How much you pay?'

He wasn't going to take me back, but at least I could go on more comfortably. In my suitcase I had packed a silver pistol; the shepherd stroked it lovingly and tucked it under his mattress.

Early next morning we lit five signal fires – a prearranged warning to our helpers at the river that we were on the last lap. We left the remaining rifles with the shepherd and set off in good spirits. My donkey was a sure-footed little beast that seemed to know the way, and we made much better progress.

Towards evening of the second day, we came out on to a rocky bluff. Three hundred feet below us, the River Araks wound through a cleft in the mountains and beyond it lay the free world. We were almost there! Juri said that his helpers had told him only to attempt the crossing in the early morning; so, for the last time, we put up our tent, made tea, and ate what was left of our rations. We were up before daybreak and, leaving all the camping gear behind, began the long climb down.

The first part was very steep and we roped together, Juri leading, then me, then the two Germans. Soon after we started there was a sudden violent storm. It became pitch dark, rain and wind lashed us, and we were in danger of being blown off the cliff. For a few minutes, we couldn't move in any direction; and then, as suddenly as it had come, the storm passed and there was just enough light in the sky to see where we were going. We were soaked to the skin and I noticed that my hands were stained reddish-brown with the dye that had run from the pockets of my suit. It didn't seem to matter very much.

Half-way down we stopped for a rest. Below us we could now see wooden watch towers, barbed wire and machine-guns – all the paraphernalia of a frontier. The second half of the descent was much easier and we unroped. The men went ahead testing the rock and showing me where to put my feet; once someone dislodged a stone and we held our breaths while it clattered downwards. Nothing happened; quietly and carefully we crept on. It was getting light now and we were each finding our own way. Osten and Wilpert had drawn well ahead, Juri was next, and I had fallen behind.

Suddenly a huge black snake slithered across my path. Involuntarily I let out a cry and jumped backwards. I fell against a boulder which detached itself and went bouncing off down the gorge like a series of thunderclaps. Dogs began to bark. I lost my head and yelled for Juri.

CHAPTER EIGHT

Last Name in the Iron Book

He was beside me in an instant, clapping his hand over my mouth. But it was too late; already the border guards were shouting up at us, and the crack of rifle fire echoed among the rocks.

Then Juri was hit; he fell across me and blood trickled from his mouth. The barking seemed to be getting nearer. I felt a sharp blow on my leg and then a strange wet warmth. Suddenly the dogs were all over us. We lay motionless, faces pressed to the ground, until the shooting died away and someone called the dogs off. In complete silence, three slit-eyed faces bent over us, the enamelled Soviet star gleaming on their caps.

Two of the soldiers carried Juri away; the third tore open a dressing and bandaged my leg; it was only then I realized I had been shot. Presently some more guards arrived with a stretcher and I was carried down to the frontier post. Juri was lying on the floor, grey-faced, with a bloody bandage round his chest. As I was carried past him to another room he managed a faint smile.

'Bye-bye, Lenotchka!'

When they put the stretcher down and left me alone, the state of shock I had been in ever since seeing the snake, suddenly broke and I started screaming. I knew it was a senseless, useless noise, but I couldn't stop. I went on and on. The sergeant on duty came in and looked at me reprovingly.

'You scream like a pig about to be slaughtered!'

I cried over and over again for Juri.

'Get that bastard in here,' the sergeant said. 'Perhaps she'll stop then.'

'It's too late, comrade,' the guard replied. 'He's dead.'

*

Later I was taken in an ambulance to the hospital at Baku where my leg was dressed.

'Bullet's gone straight through,' said the doctor approvingly. When he had finished, three men in civilian clothes came in. One of them photographed me from all angles while the other two fired questions:

'Where are the pictures?'

'What pictures?'

The man pointed at my hands. 'Don't try that on! You've been developing photographs, haven't you?'

My hands were still brown with the dye from my suit; I had no idea that developing photographs made them that colour, as I had never done any. But they didn't believe my explanation.

'What is your name?'

'Jelena Kirilovna Pushkova.'

'Come off it – your real name!'

'Jelena Pushkova, born in Lemburg, Ukraine.'

'Have it your own way. You parachuted in, I suppose?'

I didn't bother to answer.

'Tell us who your contacts are. Who were those three men?'

So Wilpert and Osten are dead too, I thought, or they would have known by now. My leg hurt and I felt the child move inside me. I closed my eyes and ignored the questions.

For a whole week I said nothing at all. They installed spotlights round my bed and questioned me day and night, I remained silent. Then one morning a different man arrived. He was alone and he drew up a chair, put his briefcase on his lap and looked me over with a mild expression.

'The doctor tells me you're much better, and the baby is all right, too. I'm really pleased about that. Let me introduce myself: my name is Bowermann and I've come all the way from

Moscow specially to see you. Now we'll have the truth, shall we? What is your name?'

'Jelena Kirilovna Pushkova.'

Bowermann smiled. 'By the way, you have a visitor.' He went over and opened the door, and two guards led Andrei into the room. He looked exhausted, unshaven and pale. I burst into tears. Andrei wasn't allowed to touch me.

'Don't worry, darling,' he said shakily. 'We'll clear everything up. I've been a member of the Party since 1938.' He patted his coat pocket. 'I have my membership book right here. We'll be free soon, you'll see.'

'That will do!' Bowermann's voice was not unfriendly. He nodded to the guards and they took Andrei away.

'Now, let's get on with it. On 16 September you left Kirovabad together with the two German engineers Wilpert and Osten, and a third man, in order to flee over the Persian border.'

'No! We were just going on a hunting trip.'

'In your condition?' Bowermann asked drily. 'Anyway, four days later your husband returned from Moscow and followed you.'

I was aghast. 'Oh no! You've got it all wrong! My husband knew nothing about it. You must believe me!'

'We shall find that out all in good time. It's you we're interested in at the moment. Who are you working for?'

'No one! I've told you. We went on a hunting trip and got lost, and the border guards opened fire on us.'

His eyes narrowed. 'Since when have German missile engineers been allowed to go hunting anywhere near the border?'

'That was our fault. We often invited them to come with us.'

'And who are "we", may I ask, since you say that your husband didn't know where you were?'

It seemed incredible that they hadn't found out who Juri was; all I could do was go on improvising. I said he was an old friend of mine from Lemburg, called Sokolenko. Bowermann opened his briefcase and handed me a crumpled piece of paper; it was one of the discarded drafts of the note I had left for Andrei, saying that Juri was my lover.

'Is that the man?'

'Yes, that's him – Juri Sokolenko.'

'When your husband was in here just now, I didn't get the impression that you had been deceiving him.' Bowermann put the letter back in his briefcase and shook his head, almost sadly.

'You're not very good at lying, are you! Shall I tell you what really happened? You were working for the Americans; I don't know how long it had been going on but we'll find out. You were well placed, with a job at the research station, and I dare say your husband discussed his work with you, too. And then for some reason you decided to leave, and you took the two Germans with you as a bonus, so to speak. This man you call Juri Sokolenko must have been your contact – but he can't have been the only one. Tell me who the others were!'

I shook my head, closing my eyes so that Bowermann should not see my relief. Evidently he didn't know very much. Andrei had not talked, and I resolved to say no more myself.

Day after day, week after week, sometimes in the middle of the night, Bowermann came and sat beside my bed. I told him nothing; I felt ill and miserable and the baby wasn't moving any more. One day I had a parcel from Kirovabad; my maid had sent some clothes for me and the child. They let me keep mine but took the baby things away, which set me off on a storm of crying. Did they, too, believe the child was dead? I cried half the night and the guard on duty in my room kept cursing in a low voice.

At last, to my delight, the movement began again, and I immediately felt better myself. But I wasn't tempted to break my silence.

Then one morning I was told to get up, a blanket was thrown over my nightdress and I was led outside to an ambulance. A nurse and one of the guards accompanied me and we drove out of Baku to an airfield, where a small aeroplane was waiting. I was helped into it and allowed to lie down on a stretcher. Then Bowermann and two KGB officers boarded the plane.

'Where are you taking me?' I asked. 'I want to stay where my husband is.'

Bowermann bent over me. 'Your husband was moved some time ago. If you wish to make a statement, I am at your disposal. Otherwise, be quiet!'

I closed my eyes. Later I gathered from the men's conversation that our destination was Moscow.

*

The city was covered in snow. I was transferred to an ambulance and sat huddled in my blanket as it sped through the cold streets. It stopped in a courtyard surrounded by high buildings, and I was led along endless corridors to a room marked 'Reception'. A woman in uniform asked if I had any complaints against my escorts. I looked at the nurse and the guard.

'No. No complaints.'

The woman signed a form and handed it to the guard, and he and the nurse left the room without a word. I felt it was time someone told me what was going on.

'Where am I, please?'

The woman stared at me with raised eyebrows. 'In prison, of course. Come on now, get undressed for your medical.'

Suddenly I realized where I was – in the Lubianka, the most notorious prison in the whole of the Soviet Union. In the time of the tsars, the Lubianka had been a luxury hotel; its history as a prison dated from the revolution. Generations of 'enemies of the people' had occupied its cells, including Lenin's old comrades-in-arms before Stalin disposed of them. Now it was a silent place, run with the smoothness of long-established routine.

I was given a bar of soap and told to take a shower; then I was issued with regulation army underwear, a brown uniform and heavy shoes. A woman doctor pronounced my condition satisfactory and finally I was allowed to rest.

After a time, a warder came for me and I was led along more corridors to a small room where an elderly woman in uniform was sitting at a table. I was told to stand with my face to the wall. Nothing happened for several minutes. Nobody spoke. I was beginning to wonder how much longer I could stand like that without fainting, when the old woman barked at me:

'Turn round and come here!'

The only thing on the table was a large book with a metal cover – the 'Iron Book' of the Lubianka. It was open, and the last name on the page was my own, with my date of birth, and, in another column, 'Committed on 10.10.1949'.

I was made to sign the entry; then the warder took me down the long corridor with the red and green lights and up in the lift to the sixth floor. In Room 656 I faced my first interrogation.

Part Two

CHAPTER NINE

A Fair Trial

That is the whole truth about how I came to be in the Lubianka. Ironically enough, it was less dangerous, to me, than the spy story they had invented; but it would have ruined Andrei and I was determined to save him if I could.

They were not unkind, that first time in Room 656. I repeated my account of the hunting trip and after an hour I was taken away. My cell was a surprise too – furnished with armchairs, a desk, a bed with white sheets and a wash-basin with hot and cold water. I was too tired to take it all in that night and fell asleep instantly. In the morning Bowermann came to see me.

'How are you, my dear? The accommodation isn't bad, is it? You can see that in the Soviet Union we know how to treat prisoners properly.'

I thought of the camp at Novosibirsk and said nothing. Bowermann, all smiles, took pencil and paper from his briefcase and arranged them on the desk.

'Now then. Just sit down here and write out a complete confession. Name your employers and your contacts; the more you write the better for you. If you need anything – here's the telephone, you've only to pick up the receiver.'

For four days I was well fed and considerately treated; almost, apart from the lack of freedom, like a guest in a hotel. I knew perfectly well that information was expected in return, but the sheets of paper remained blank. When Bowermann came back, he was furious; it was the first time he had lost his temper with me. In a way it was almost a relief to discover that he had human feelings. I was taken back to the interrogation room and subjected to a much rougher questioning, with bright spotlights, threats and abuse. The head of the investigating panel was a man with red hair and cat-like green eyes; he seized me by the shoulders and shook me violently, shouting, 'If you weren't pregnant, I'd break every bone in your bloody body!'

After that, I fainted. A doctor tended me with sterile indifference and I was returned to my cell.

Over the next few weeks I was kept constantly on the move. Sometimes I shared a communal cell with criminals and prostitutes; sometimes I was in solitary confinement. The interrogations took place without warning at any time of the day or night. The questions were always the same, and so were the promises – freedom as soon as I told the truth. I didn't believe them and felt no inclination to weaken.

One day the red-haired man put a prepared confession in front of me and told me to sign it. When I refused he hit me in the face with his fist and made my nose bleed. It was the first real violence I had been offered and my reaction was blind rage. I called for pencil and paper and wrote a note threatening to complain about my treatment as soon as I was released. It was an absurd gesture; I had no hope of release – and there was nobody in all Russia to whom one could make such a complaint.

There were no more interrogations. Instead I was left in solitary confinement for weeks on end. Twice a day food was brought; occasionally a woman doctor would come and examine me; much of the time I wept with loneliness. Then at last, one afternoon in December, another bed was pushed into the cell. I was to have company.

A girl I knew was carried in, a young Jewess called Shoura who had been particularly kind to me when we were together in a communal cell. She was unconscious and blood seeped from the corner of her mouth. I sponged her swollen face as best I could, and after a time she moved a little. I asked her what on earth had happened.

'They beat me,' she whispered, but the effort made her cough and spit blood. I made her drink a spoonful of water and then left her to sleep.

She lay there for two days, and on the third evening she

was taken away for another interrogation. Early next morning a stretcher was carried in. I could only recognize Shoura by her black hair. As I knelt helplessly beside her, light red blood suddenly gushed from what remained of her nose and mouth. I hammered on the cell door and shouted, and presently the woman doctor hurried in with two warders. Shoura was covered with a blanket and taken away.

In the silence that followed, I went berserk. I banged my tin mug against the door and yelled, 'Murderers! Beasts! Criminals!' at the top of my voice. It was as futile as any other protest in that place, but I didn't care; my sanity hung by a thread. They came and slapped my face to make me stop; then they took the pins out of my hair, cut the metal buttons off my clothes, and put me in a small, rubber-walled cell in total darkness.

I have no idea how long I was there. From time to time there was a chink of light as the door opened and bread and water were pushed in. Otherwise I just sat in the dark, unable to tell night from day. When at last they came for me, I was too stiff with cold to get up, and had to be half-carried to the lift. But then, to my astonishment, I was put to bed in the luxurious cell I had occupied when I first arrived. It was all completely baffling.

A few days later Bowermann came to see me, immaculate in uniform instead of the drab civilian clothes he usually wore. His eyes fastened on my half-open prison blouse.

'You look enchanting, my dear. I'm so glad to see you are well again.'

'I'm not well at all!' I retorted furiously. 'I can't stop thinking about Shoura.'

'Who on earth is Shoura?'

'One of your prisoners. She was battered to death. She died in my cell.'

'Oh yes,' he said casually, 'I remember now. Is that what all the fuss was about?'

I jumped up and hit him in the face. The blow couldn't have hurt him much, but it wiped off the veneer of friendliness. He seized my wrists and forced me back into my chair.

'Stop that, you silly bitch! Don't you realize this is your last chance? Give me the names of your contacts, and you will be free tomorrow. Otherwise . . .'

'Otherwise, what?'

Bowermann shook his head reproachfully. 'Hasn't anyone told you? Your case comes up for trial in three days' time.'

So that was why I was suddenly so comfortable and well fed! I was even issued with new and reasonably becoming clothes of warm grey flannel; it was evidently important that a prisoner appearing in public should be a credit to the system.

When I was led into the court room on the first morning of the trial, I was horrified to find that Andrei was in the dock too; we were in separate wooden boxes on opposite sides of the room. He looked terrible; his head was like a skull, shorn of hair, the grey skin taut over jutting cheekbones. Instinctively I moved towards him and held out my arms; a warder pulled me back and ordered me to be quiet. Andrei wouldn't look at me. I sat crying helplessly until the judges were announced and we all had to stand up.

Andrei and I had to remain standing while a clerk read out the indictment. It took a very long time, and towards the end my knees began to buckle and I had to be supported by the warder. The prosecution's case against me was virtually the same as the confession that Bowermann had been trying for so long to make me sign. Andrei was accused of having known of my plan to escape and done nothing to stop me; alternatively, of trying to escape himself. At last, as the expressionless voice droned on, he lifted his head and our eyes met across the packed court room.

When the clerk sat down, the presiding judge addressed me.

'Are you the wife of the accused Sidrov?'

'Yes.'

'Kindly tell the court how and why you made this attempt to escape on 16th September.'

For what seemed like the thousandth time, I repeated my story of the hunting trip.

'What was this man Juri Sokolenko doing in Kirovabad?'

'He was staying with us because there was famine in the Ukraine.'

'Be silent!' the judge snapped. 'There is no famine anywhere in the Soviet Union! And if you were out hunting, why had you no guns?'

'They were stolen while we were asleep. And then we lost the way, and we only realized we were close to the border when the guards opened fire.'

'Stop insulting the court with your fairy tales!' It was the chief prosecutor, purple with rage, thumping the table with his fist.

I had been on my feet for some time and at that moment I fainted. When I came to, I was in bed in a small room with a woman doctor in attendance, and there I remained for the rest of the day while the trial went on without me.

Next morning, a number of officers from the Kirovabad missile base were waiting in court to give evidence. Among them I noticed Lieutenant-Colonel Abramov, my former boss, and Major Pavlov, an extraordinarily handsome man who had been something of a heartthrob among the station wives. Further along the line sat Lieutenant-Colonel Zarubkin, Andrei's deputy, and I felt sick with dread when I saw him. Not only would he be after Andrei's job, but he had good reason to dislike us both – and this, like so much else, was all my fault. He and his wife had been close friends of ours once, but Zarubkin had become attracted to me and I had done nothing to discourage him. It had all ended in a dreadful scene, during which I had called his plain, stout wife a 'jealous hippo'. Since then, we hadn't been on speaking terms, and I felt sure he had come to take his revenge.

No sooner had the judges arrived, than nausea overcame me and I had to be taken out. It was decided that I need not attend the hearing of the witnesses, and I was allowed to lie down. But after a little while I couldn't bear not knowing what was being said about me and insisted on going back.

Lieutenant-Colonel Abramov was being questioned. He was standing rigidly upright, staring at the picture of Stalin on the wall behind the judges' bench. The prosecutor had just finished asking him whether the German engineers, Wilpert and Osten, had taken anything from the base when they left.

'No.'

'How long was it before the accused Sidrov returned from Moscow?'

'We informed Colonel Sidrov . . .'

'Don't call the accused "Colonel"!' interrupted the prosecutor.

'On our recommendation,' Abramov continued, 'the accused cut short his official trip and was back four days later.'

'The accused Pushkova worked in the design department of the base under your supervision. Did you ever notice anything about her behaviour that might have warned you of her spying activities?'

Abramov glanced quickly at me and then resumed his contemplation of Stalin.

'The accused Pushkova was a good interpreter. I never noticed anything out of the ordinary in her behaviour.'

That was the end of Abramov's testimony. The next witness was Major Pavlov.

'What was your relationship with the accused Pushkova?'

Pavlov, slim and elegant, frowned at the prosecutor. 'I don't think I understand your question.'

'I am asking you whether you often saw her privately, outside working hours.'

'No, I did not. But I enjoyed dancing with her at official parties.'

'Did the accused ever question you or show particular interest in missile technology?'

'Not that I remember. But there were times when I needed her help in communicating with the German engineers. Naturally we were dealing with technical matters.'

The prosecutor leaned forward conspiratorially. 'Do you believe that the accused was practising espionage at the missile base?'

Pavlov looked thoroughly indignant. He stared straight at me and answered in a firm voice, 'No! I would never believe that!'

Then it was Zarubkin's turn. My heart pounded as he took the oath, and I waited for him to destroy us. Calmly, the prosecutor began his examination.

'Lieutenant-Colonel Zarubkin, you were the deputy of the accused Sidrov?'

'Yes, I was.'

'When you telephoned him in Moscow to tell him about his wife's disappearance, did he instruct you to look for the two Germans?'

'No, he said nothing about them. The colonel was frantic with worry about...'

'Don't call the accused "Colonel"!' the judge interrupted. Zarubkin bowed slightly, and the prosecutor continued.

'What happened when the accused returned to the base?'

'He called for his car and drove out into the mountains.'

'Did he not order an alert?'

'No.'

'Didn't that arouse your suspicions?'

'No, because I assumed that he had agreed a plan of action with the authorities in Moscow. When he had not come back by the next morning, I telephoned them, and subsequently ordered a full alert. The accused was then arrested in the mountains by security agents. He said that he had been looking for his wife and the two Germans.' Zarubkin looked at Andrei as if inviting him to confirm the statement, but Andrei remained staring into space.

Then the second prosecutor got up.

'Lieutenant-Colonel Zarubkin, you had to deal with the accused Pushkova in the execution of your duties. Did you never have any suspicions that she might be a spy?'

'If I had, I would have informed Central Office straight away.'

'What central office are you talking about?'

'The KGB. I am the base security officer and it's my duty to report anything in the least suspicious.'

'Would you give the court a brief assessment of the accused, please.'

'Her translation work was excellent,' said Zarubkin after a slight pause. 'Her behaviour was correct at all times, and by her industry she set an example to the rest of our civilian personnel.'

'Were you on friendly terms with the accused?'

'For a time, my wife and I saw a lot of the accused Sidrov and the accused Pushkova. But then, as so often happens, our wives quarrelled and the friendship came to an end.'

Zarubkin looked straight across at me as he spoke and I could feel myself blushing with embarrassment and shame. I had expected a vindictive testimony; instead, he had been as kind and generous as possible.

CHAPTER TEN

Labour Pains

During the lunch adjournment I felt absolutely confident that both Andrei and I would be acquitted. Nothing had been proved against us; none of the witnesses had said an unfavourable word. It could only be a matter of hours now before we were together again, and free. I walked back into the court room almost jauntily.

The afternoon was taken up with long speeches by prosecuting counsel, followed by short ones by the defence. The prosecutor demanded sentences of twenty-five years' hard labour for each of us; whereupon a defence lawyer whom I, at any rate, had never seen before, drew the judge's attention to Andrei's distinguished army career, and to my youth and pregnancy. I could hardly believe my ears; everyone was behaving as they they still thought we were guilty!

Finally, Andrei and I were each allowed to say once more that I was not a spy and then the judges retired to consider their verdict. I spent an hour in a small waiting room; tea and sandwiches were provided but I couldn't swallow anything, and when I was taken back into court I was shaking so much I could hardly stand.

The presiding judge read out a long statement in a fast, monotonous voice. He repeated everything the prosecutor had accused us of, and then he came to Andrei's sentence – ten years in a labour camp and three years' loss of citizenship. There was a sudden roaring in my ears and I lost consciousness.

When I came to, I was in bed and the woman doctor was bending over me.

'Pull yourself together,' she said brusquely, 'or you'll miss the chance of seeing your husband!' Then she went to the door and opened it. 'You can bring him in now.'

Andrei was deathly pale and breathing heavily. He kissed me, and we clung together for a moment.

'Don't lose hope my darling,' he murmured, 'I'll appeal against the verdicts and we'll win, I'm sure.'

Tears were pouring down my face. 'Andrei, it was all my fault! I'm sorry! I'm so sorry! Can you forgive me?'

'It will be all right. Don't worry. Just take care of yourself and the baby. I shall always think of you both.'

Then the guards took him away. I had forgotten to ask him what my own sentence was.

*

The red-haired commandant at the Lubianka told me it was six years, and added his opinion that I was very lucky to have got off so lightly. It sounded like an eternity to me, and I lay sobbing on my hard bunk all night. By a coincidence, it was Christmas Eve again, though no one would have known it there.

On 28 December I was moved to the Butirka, one of the largest, oldest and gloomiest prisons in the whole of Russia. Cell 81, to which I was taken, reminded me vividly of the bladnoias' hut in Novosibirsk. There was the same fetid reek as the door was opened, and I was overcome with nausea and misery. Had I really got to live through all that again?

The cell was designed for thirty inmates, but it held more than twice that number. I could find nowhere to lie down; finally a young woman took pity on me and invited me to share her piece of floor. At four o'clock each morning, a hundred women fought for the use of five lavatories and five cold water taps; and for fifteen minutes each day we walked round the prison yard. For the rest of the time I lay or crouched on the bare, filthy boards, until on the fourth day I began to have labour pains.

*

There were about twenty of us in the maternity ward. It was such luxury to be in a bed again that I went immediately to sleep – to be woken later by loud laughter and singing. My companions, unkempt women in the last few days of pregnancy, were dancing and prancing round the ward brandishing bottles of vodka and singing bawdy songs. I pulled the bedclothes over my head, but there was no escape from the ridiculous, horrifying scene.

'Come and join us, love! We might as well have fun while we can. We're celebrating the New Year!'

A ravishingly pretty girl with black hair and blue eyes was sitting on my bed. She ignored my protests and handed me a mug of vodka.

'Go on, drink up! My name's Zena. What's yours?' I told her. 'What have you done?'

'I'm political.'

'Aha – then you're the most dangerous of us all! Never mind, drink this and forget your worries.'

It was good vodka and I soon began to feel quite cheerful. Zena told me that the other women were all petty criminals of one sort or another. She herself had been convicted of murder, which gave her a certain standing among them; also, it was an admirer of hers who had smuggled in the vodka. As we all got to know each other I found that my situation commanded even more respect – I was a political prisoner, the wife of a colonel, and, most extraordinary of all, I made the effort to wash all over every day.

My first pains had been a false alarm, but the doctor let me stay in the ward and on 4 January I went into labour in earnest. All the women gathered round my bed. But I was taken to the labour room and left alone on a cold, rubber-covered table. During the night, Zena brought me some blankets, but in the morning the midwife took them away, complaining that they were not sterile. Zena promptly brought them back again and terrified the midwife into letting me keep them and the next night she brought me tea and honey. By then I was very weak and again it was Zena who found the doctor and insisted that something was done for me. I was given an injection, and at last, on 6 January, 1950, my son was born. It was Christmas

Day of the Orthodox Church and bells were ringing all over Moscow.

Four days later, Zena gave birth to a girl, and we were together in the nursery with our babies. There were times, as I lay in the clean bright room with little Alik in my arms, that I felt almost happy.

When we were up, Zena was put to work in the prison kitchen and soon had the cook running after her; it was the supply chief she really had her eye on. I had enough milk for both babies and was quite content with my job in the kindergarten while Zena pursued her aims. Once her mother came to see her, to discuss a petition for clemency. I didn't know there was such a thing.

'Where does one send it?'

'To Comrade Shvernik, Chairman of the Praesidium of the Supreme Soviet. But your relatives outside have to do it.'

'I haven't got any.'

'Oh dear!' Zena frowned. 'I'll have to think about that. There must be something you can do.'

She was an amazing girl. Her own sentence was for twenty-five years, and yet she seemed more worried about me than about herself. In fact, she seemed absolutely confident that she would get out soon.

'Plenty of people owe me a favour,' she laughed. 'Meanwhile, I'll apply to go to the Meeting House.'

'What's that?'

'You don't know anything, do you! It's where we can spend a day or two with our lovers or husbands – if we've been good and if they're not in prison themselves.'

'I don't believe it!'

'Don't be silly. How did you imagine all those women got pregnant? Some of them have been inside for years!'

In due course Zena was given a clean prison dress and taken away. She came back three days later looking sleek and smug.

'He was even allowed to see the baby!' she chortled. 'He adores it – and he wants to marry me!'

Three weeks later she received another pass for the Meeting House. This time she took the child with her, and all her things, and she never came back. I often wondered whether she had been very lucky, or very unlucky. It could have been either. I never heard from her again.

*

Soon after Zena had disappeared, a warder woke me in the middle of the night and told me to follow him, just as in the old days in the Lubianka. Just as in the old days, Bowermann was waiting in the interrogation room. He laughed when he saw my astonishment.

'Did you think we had forgotten about you? We never forget anyone, my dear.'

I smiled wanly back. Somehow I knew he wouldn't hurt me, although now that I wasn't pregnant there was no knowing what the others might do. I remembered Shoura and shuddered. Bowermann was holding out his hand.

'Congratulations on the birth of your son!'

'Thank you.'

'In the meantime, we have found out that you are a German national.'

I said nothing. It might be a trap.

'Before we start a new investigation, I advise you to tell me who you are and who was your contact. You only need to name one agent and you will be free immediately.'

It was all too horribly familiar. The questions, promises and threats went on for three hours and then I was led, exhausted, back to the nursery. I couldn't sleep, but lay wondering how they knew so much. Had Andrei been tortured? The possibility froze my blood.

Next morning I was taken to an isolation block for political prisoners. Bowermann came to my cell and put pencil and paper on the table.

'I'll give you a week. Write everything down and then we'll release you.'

I waited in silence until he went away.

The isolation block wasn't bad; my cell was warm and clean and there was plenty of food. During the day I worked in the library with an elderly prisoner called Valentina. She drew my attention to the small table at which I was sitting.

'Dora Kaplan usually works there, you know!'

'Who is she?'

Valentina was appalled. 'You mean to say you don't know! She tried to assassinate Lenin!'

'But she can't be still alive!'

'Yes. Lenin commuted her death sentence. She has been here for almost thirty years. She's sick at the moment. We regard it as an honour to work at her table.'

I wasn't impressed; it was all too long ago, and I was pining for Alik. From now on, they said, I could only see him on Sundays. My breasts, full of milk, hurt all the time.

*

At the end of the week Bowermann came back and was furious to find I had written nothing.

'I told you – I have nothing to confess.'

'You'll do it in the end, believe me!'

That same day, I was moved back to a communal cell. It had no bunks; the floor was covered in rotting straw and the only light was a small lamp which burned day and night. The other women were all filthy, tattooed creatures like the bladnoias of Novosibirsk, and the work we had to do was as bad as any there. We were the underground tunnelling unit. At six each morning we were taken in a truck already half full of male prisoners, to a place where the men dug up the frozen ground and the women carried loads of rails and sleepers. After eight hours of labour we were returned to our cell, and there was no humanity anywhere. On the journey to and fro, the men and women hurled obscenities at each other. The food ration was half a pound of bread and a bowl of cabbage soup, each day. I was always hungry, always tired; my back and my breasts ached intolerably, and at night the bugs in the straw woke up and made sleep impossible.

Somehow I got through the week, in order to see Alik on Sunday. At the nursery, one of the staff met me.

'Your baby is ill, comrade.'

He was lying quietly in his cot. I picked him up and kissed him. His forehead was burning hot and he didn't seem to know I was there. I went back to the cell stupefied with misery. Next evening after work I was called to the sick-room. The woman doctor told me he had diphtheria and it might be too

81

late to save him. I knelt and flung my arms round the cot where
he lay motionless.

'I won't go back tonight! I must stay with him – please!'

In the end I was allowed to stay, and for hours I listened to
the faint breathing and his little feverish moans. Then there
was a sudden silence. Alik's face was blue. I jumped up and
shouted until a doctor came – a man this time. He examined
the baby carefully and then covered his body with a cloth.

'Meningitis,' he said, 'I'm sorry.'

I snatched the cloth away. 'No, he's not dead. I won't have it!
You've got to save him!'

The doctor looked at me through his steel-rimmed glasses.

'I could try a lumbar puncture, but it's dangerous in a child
that age, you understand.'

'Never mind – try it!'

Afterwards I was allowed to stay another day.

'His chances are very slim,' the doctor said, 'but if you
could breast-feed him, it would help.'

By the evening Alik did seem a little better, but I was
ordered back to the tunnelling squad and had to do a full day's
work before I could see him again. Next evening, to my horror,
I found him lying on the bare floor.

'I'm sorry,' said the woman doctor, 'the cot was needed for
another child who might recover. I don't really think your little
boy has much chance.'

The doctor turned away and I was taken back to the cell.
Next day in the tunnel an old newspaper blew past and auto-
matically I grabbed it; it would do to pad my boots. On the
front page there was a photograph of a baby lying in a chest
drawer, and the caption read: 'No cot for a worker's baby in
capitalist England!' Below it was an article about the hardships
endured by the working classes in the West.

My mood of despair gave way to one of blind rage. How
could such stupidity exist? What wouldn't I give to see Alik
snugly tucked up in a drawer! Did no one in Russia know what
was going on?

As soon as we got back to the prison after work, I said I
wanted to make a confession. Pencil and paper were hurriedly
brought. I wrote two letters; one was an appeal to Comrade
Shvernik, enclosing the picture of the English baby; the other

was to the commandant of the Butirka prison asking permission to stay with my sick child. I hid the first letter in my quilted jacket, and asked the warder to deliver the second.

The brigadier in charge of the tunnelling squad was an ugly, decent man who had occasionally shown me some kindness – a piece of bread, or a drag on a cigarette. At work next day I asked him point-blank if he would post my letter to Shvernik. He didn't like it, but I only had to cry a little, and he said he would.

CHAPTER ELEVEN

An Important Appointment

Four days later, instead of going to work in the tunnel, we were told to scrub out our cell. Sacks of fresh straw were distributed, and then we were taken to the showers. My vest was sticky with milk and crawling with lice, but I didn't have to put it back on as we were all issued with clean underwear. In the afternoon I was taken to see the commandant. He asked after my health and I told him I was worried to death about Alik.

'Don't give up hope,' he said kindly. 'Your son is still alive and the doctors are doing all they can. It might be best if you moved back into the nursery ward.'

Neither of us mentioned my letter, and, indeed, it may have had nothing to do with it, because the next day a commission came to inspect the Butirka. There were five men and two women, and the commandant's job depended upon their good report. They trooped into the nursery sick-room wearing snow-white overalls and face masks, and they spent some time bending over Alik – now back in a cot, with clean sheets. Then their appraising eyes looked me up and down.

'Have you any complaints?'

'No, not really. If I can just stay with my child.'

'Naturally. Have you enough milk to feed him?'

'Yes.'

'Excellent!' The inspection party swept out again.

For everybody else in the prison, life returned to normal as soon as they had gone, but I was allowed to stay in the nursery. Alik was too weak to suck for more than a few seconds at a time, so I fed him every half-hour, day and night. I was willing him to live, and gradually my hopes rose.

*

On 13 March, I was woken early, taken to have a bath, and issued with clean clothes. Then my hair was shampooed and set in curls.

'What's happening?' I asked the nurse. 'I'm not going anywhere without Alik!' She assured me I would be back in the evening.

At ten o'clock, two KGB officers came for me and we drove into Moscow in the prison van. Nothing was explained. We stopped outside a large yellowish building and I was escorted along vast corridors of pink marble. One of the officers produced a red card, and this was stamped at various stages on our route. We passed through marble halls where people stood about whispering and waiting, and finally reached a broad staircase. A clerk produced a file which one of my escorts tucked under his arm, and we went on up the stairs. On the next floor, thick red carpet muffled our footsteps, and there was no one about. Presently we came to a door flanked by two armed guards. They looked at our documents, and let us in.

A major rose and pushed a book across an enormous desk.

'Please write your name here.'

It was the first time anyone had spoken to me. He was a friendly-looking man of about thirty-five; and after he had taken the file and dismissed the two escorts, he offered me a cigarette. I was trembling so much I could hardly hold it. Then the telephone rang.

'Yes, she's here.'

Another door opened and a man in civilian clothes told us to come in. The next room was unbelievably splendid; crystal chandeliers hung from a marble ceiling; priceless oriental carpets covered the floor; everything was on a huge scale. In the middle of it all, behind a mammoth desk covered with telephones, sat an old man in a dark suit. He looked at me gravely for a few minutes. Then he told us to sit down, and asked me for my name. I had to clear my throat before I could answer.

He nodded slowly, but his eyes were shrewd.

'Do you know who I am?' I shook my head. 'I am Chairman Shvernik.'

Involuntarily I stood up again. He smiled.

'Do please sit down! I have sent for you because of this letter. It is yours, isn't it?' He held it out to me, and I nodded. He took out the newspaper cutting and looked at it closely.

'What exactly is it that annoys you about this photograph?'

I glanced up at Shvernik and there seemed to be something like genuine interest in his eyes; well, he should have an honest answer.

'When I saw the picture, my own child was lying on the bare floor of a prison, desperately ill, and I thought, instead of maligning the West, it would be better . . . '

The nameless civilian jumped to his feet and cut me short.

'What is the West to you? Are you trying to make trouble?'

'Of course not! I only . . . '

'Shut up! You ought to be ashamed of yourself. No Soviet citizen should talk like that!'

'But I am not a Soviet citizen!' I cried, and burst into tears. The nice major passed me a handkerchief, and all three men watched in silence while I blew my nose.

The civilian had a long scar on his cheek which had turned red while he was shouting at me. When he spoke again, the scar had faded and his voice was quiet and rational.

'In your letter you wrote that you would only confess to Comrade Shvernik himself. So how about it? You'll never get a chance like this again.'

I hesitated, not knowing how to begin. Then Chairman Shvernik leaned across his great desk and smiled.

'Tell us everything, little German girl!'

So I did. I talked for over an hour and no one interrupted me. It was a wonderful relief to be telling the truth without attempting to hide any part of it. At the end I said,

'I know I have made many mistakes but the only thing really on my conscience is the fact that my husband was convicted because of me. I only tried to escape to avoid getting him into trouble. I swear, as I have always sworn, that he knew nothing about it and that I was never a spy.' Then I looked straight at Shvernik.

'I don't care what you do to me, Comrade Chairman. I only beg you to help my son.'

'Where is the child now?' he wanted to know, 'and how is he?'

The meeting was adjourned for lunch. I was given sandwiches in the ante-room, and later I had to go back into Shvernik's office and supply the addresses of everyone I had mentioned. The scarred man was there, with a stranger. I hesitated over Sonya's address.

'Why do you want that? You won't arrest her?'

'We have to check your statement. If it's true, nothing will happen to anyone.' Miserably, I gave them the addresses.

'Thank you,' the scarred man said. 'You needn't feel guilty. We would have got them anyway. It's just quicker like this.'

Shvernik came round from behind his desk and put his hand on my shoulder.

'If you have told us the truth, my dear, you will be given an amnesty; this is my personal promise.' He indicated the man with the scar. 'Comrade Abakumov will have your statement checked and then he will tell you what is to be done with you in future. One thing you will be pleased about – your son is to be treated in a Moscow children's clinic. I hope he will be better soon. I wish you luck.'

Comrade Abakumov didn't know how to smile. 'First, you will stay at the clinic with your son,' he said. 'In all other respects, Major Tshernikov will look after you.'

Without thinking, I flung my arms round his neck and kissed him. The major led me away, and as soon as we were outside the door he burst out laughing.

'What's so funny?'

'I don't suppose,' he said between convulsions, 'that many prisoners have kissed the Minister for State Security!'

After that, Major Tshernikov took me shopping. He only had to show his red card and all the assistants rushed to serve us and to bring out their best goods. Soon, I was dressed as smartly as any wealthy Muscovite could be in those days, and we were both loaded with parcels. I was in a happy dream as we walked back to the car.

'Are we going to the clinic now?'

'I don't think there's any hurry; your boy's there and he's in good hands. Aren't you hungry?'

'I'm always hungry!'

He directed the driver to a famous restaurant where we dined to the music of a gypsy band. Afterwards, lingering over our wine, Tshernikov ran through the details of my new life.

'You'll keep the name Pushkova for the time being; it's simpler for everybody. You will be sharing a room at the clinic with two other women. If they ask you about your husband, say he's on a business trip to Vladivostok.'

'Why?'

'Why? Do you want to explain that your husband . . . '

'No, no, of course not! I'm sorry!'

'I shall come and visit you quite frequently, on the instructions of Comrade Abakumov. I must say,' he grinned, 'this is one of the nicest orders I've ever been given! But again, if anyone asks you, say I'm your husband's brother.'

'All right.'

He refilled our glasses. 'And now we must drink to a closer relationship. If I am to be your brother-in-law, we can't stay on such formal terms. My name is Michael Petrovitch, and my friends call me Misha.' He raised his glass towards me.

'*Nasdarovie*, Jelena!'

'*Nasdarovie*, Misha!'

Later, during the drive to the clinic, he kissed me. I didn't mind.

When we got there he demanded to see my son. It wasn't visiting time, but once again his red card removed all obstacles and we were both taken to see the sleeping child. He looked so comfortable.

'What is his name?' Misha whispered.

'Alexander – Alik for short.'

'Alexander the Small! Just look how tiny his fingers are!'

'You're behaving as if you'd never seen a baby before!'

'Well, to tell the truth, I haven't. Not from so close, anyway. I am a bachelor after all!'

*

Two days later Misha brought a stranger to see me, whom he introduced as his friend Pavel Antonovich Sudoplatov. Both men were in civilian clothes and laden with presents for Alik and me. There was something odd about Sudoplatov; he hardly spoke, but stared at me quite rudely throughout the visit. Also, he seemed much too old to be Misha's friend; but when I saw Misha alone next day he refused to discuss him.

*

We stayed in the clinic for four weeks, and then came the day I both longed for and dreaded, when the doctors pronounced Alik fit. What would happen to us now? I waited anxiously for Misha's visit; but when he came he already knew that we were being discharged and he was in high spirits.

'But where am I to go, Misha?'

'To your new flat, of course! I'll come and fetch you at ten o'clock tomorrow morning.'

The flat was on the second floor of an apartment block on Gorki Embankment – living room, bathroom, kitchenette and balcony. It was completely furnished, even to a bright red pram. Misha opened the door to the balcony and let in the mild spring air.

'Well – how do you like it?'

My first reaction had of course been one of incredulous delight; now I felt the first twinge of fear.

'It's lovely. But why are you doing all this?'

His eyes were fixed on the ceiling. 'Don't ask too many questions, Jelena.'

'Oh Misha, I'm frightened! I know this country a little bit now. Nobody gets anything for nothing.'

'Rubbish! Anyway, I'm only carrying out orders. I was told to look after you, and I am.' He put his hands on my shoulders. 'And I'm getting very fond of you in the process.'

I turned my head away from his kiss. 'Don't forget I'm married!'

'I never do,' he answered sadly. 'There's nothing any of us can do to help your husband, but I hope someone will tell him that you and Alik are all right. Try not to worry about him too much.'

'Well then, why am I here?'

'If you must know, we are hoping you will work for us.'

'The KGB?'

'Yes. It's a great honour, you know.'

'And if I won't?'

Misha pulled me down on to the sofa and put his arms round me. 'It's like this, Lenotchka. There's an outstanding labour camp sentence of nine years, and a prison sentence of nearly six years waiting to be served. You don't want to put the clock back, do you?'

I realized I would do absolutely anything to keep my liberty.

CHAPTER TWELVE

First Assignment

Ten days later I began my new career. Alik went to stay with Misha's mother, who was delighted to have a baby to look after again; and Misha drove me to a gaunt building that made me shy like a frightened horse.

'But this is the Lubianka! I'm not going in there!'

He laughed. 'I'm afraid you must. We've done a lot for you, but you can't expect us to move our headquarters!'

In Room 540 a man in the uniform of a general, with the blue KGB stripes on his shoulder straps, got up to welcome me. It was Misha's 'friend' Sudoplatov. He smiled at my surprise and handed me a form to fill in.

'Please complete this questionnaire as fully as you can. Comrade Tshernikov will help you with it.'

I was ushered back to the ante-room before I could say a word. There were twenty-four questions to answer, covering not only my own life but that of my family as well. Two hours later I signed the form and Misha took it into the general's office. For several minutes I could just hear their murmuring voices and I felt sure they were deciding to reject me. Too many relatives abroad, perhaps, or my service in the Girls' Hitler Youth. I was almost resigned to being locked up again when Misha opened the door.

'Come in please, comrade.'

General Sudoplatov was grinning broadly. 'This is great, really great! Polish, Ukrainian and German as foreign

91

languages, and youth and beauty as well!' His eyes wandered over me with obvious relish. 'We've been looking for someone like you for a long time.'

I fidgeted with embarrassment and the general became brisk and businesslike again.

'Joining the Service is entirely voluntary, of course. Here in the Soviet Union we would never force anyone to take such a job.'

I knew it was useless, but something made me say, 'In that case, comrade General, I don't think I will take it. I'd rather go back to Germany.'

Misha gasped and the general's head jerked back as if I had slapped him. When he spoke his voice had a steady edge to it.

'Kindly be more realistic about your situation. Either you work for us or you complete your prison sentences. You have a free choice – but there are no other alternatives.'

I bowed my head.

Misha took me to the clothing store where I was issued with the uniform of a lieutenant in the KGB, olive drab with blue piping, well-cut and attractive. My photograph was taken; and to my horror I was given a pistol. A young Army captain spent two hours trying to teach me to use it. The mechanics were no problem; I could soon dismantle and reassemble it quickly; but I couldn't fire it without flinching. As we left, the young man said to Misha, 'She'll never master it, you know.' I had already decided that firearms were not for me.

At last I stood again before General Sudoplatov, in uniform and armed. He handed me my red card and looked me over from all angles.

'Marvellous! Fantastic! It's exactly how I imagined you would look. What an impression this is going to make abroad! But first I have a surprise for you. Have you ever seen our beloved Comrade Stalin?' I shook my head. 'You shall see him on your first assignment. We are sending you and Comrade Tshernikov to the May Day celebrations at the Kremlin. Report to the Minister for briefing at ten o'clock tomorrow morning.'

As we were driving home I appealed to Misha, 'Will I ever get out of this again?'

'I shouldn't think so.' Then he stared at me in genuine

amazement. 'Why would you ever want to get out? It's an honourable and interesting career and the pay is generous. Alik has a good home with my mother and you can see him whenever you like. It's an ideal arrangement; what's the matter?'

'You must have worked all that out with the general in advance, I suppose?'

'Yes, of course. We don't leave things to chance. But I must say it suits me very well, too!'

'Misha, do you think the general could do anything for my husband?'

The smile was wiped off his face, and his voice grew hard. 'No, he can't, and if he could, he wouldn't. I've told you before, you must put him out of your mind.'

I was angry with myself for trying to rush things. It was far too soon to try to help Andrei. First, I had to prove myself as a secret service agent, and that would be quite difficult enough.

*

'The uniform suits you,' said Comrade Abakumov next morning. 'Please sit down. I congratulate you on joining the Security Service. Your file is in our safe; nobody else must ever know that you are German. You're a Soviet citizen from the Ukraine, understand?' I nodded, and he continued. 'For the time being, your duties will be largely social. You will attend receptions, concerts, events of that sort where foreign visitors are expected. You will act as hostess to official delegations, and sometimes you may be instructed to get on friendly terms with a particular individual. Later, you will represent the Soviet Union at similar functions abroad. On each occasion you will submit a written report on everything you have seen and heard.'

'I'm not sure I can do all that, Comrade Minister. Surely a genuine Russian woman . . . '

He raised his hand. 'Our women are hard workers and good communists; but when foreign visitors are off-duty they don't want to hear any more about communism. They are looking for feminine charm and affection – which you will be able to offer them. Do you understand now, Jelena Kirilovna?'

Over the intercom he ordered a bottle of champagne and three glasses, and told Misha to come in.

'We drink to your future, Comrade Pushkova. And now for your first mission.'

He briefed us on the Labour Day reception.

*

Misha and I attended as husband and wife. We mixed first with the German delegates; their behaviour was exceedingly correct and polite, but after a time their fulsome praise of everything Russian became monotonous. I was wedged among them, when somebody said, 'Look, here comes Comrade Stalin!'

And so it was that, ten years after Helga Wannenmacher had come face to face with Hitler, Jelena Pushkova shook hands with Stalin. It was all over in a moment. He said a few words to me which I didn't catch, as the Germans round me were all clapping excitedly, but I still remember the feeling of his papery old hand in mine.

As soon as the Germans began filling their plates at the buffet, I slipped away and joined the other group we had been told to mingle with, the Poles. They were much more fun – particularly a certain Major Stanislaus Boshinski, who had discovered that there was dancing going on in another of the great Kremlin halls and was delighted to find a partner. He was handsome, amusing and a wonderful dancer, and I could easily have forgotten why I was there, had I not seen, every now and then, Abakumov's pale, scarred face in a corner, watching me.

'I shall be in Moscow for another week,' said Major Boshinski at the end of the evening. 'It would be a great pleasure if I could see you and your husband again.'

We arranged to meet at the Bolshoi the following evening, after the parade in Red Square. It was a long and tiring day, and on the way home I asked Misha if I need really go to the theatre.

'Of course you must; it's duty. This Boshinski fellow is tying himself in knots over you and we might well find out something from him. We'll ask him back to your flat for a drink afterwards.'

'I don't understand! The Poles are not enemies; they're our allies. What could we possibly find out?'

'We want to know how genuine their communism is; whether there's any American influence; that sort of thing.'

'But Misha, if we trust our friends so little, we must distrust each other as well!'

He laughed. 'We do, Lenotchka, we do. You'll soon find out. KGB agents must trust nobody. Our work begins with searching waste paper baskets and ends with . . . well, in your case, darling, it may end in somebody's bed. All in the interests of the communist party, you understand.'

*

Major Boshinski was such a nice man I felt sure he couldn't be an American agent, but I was nervous that if Misha filled him up with drink he might say something that would land him in the Lubianka. During the first interval I went to the Ladies and scribbled a note in Polish with my eyebrow pencil: 'Keep away from us.' The major squeezed my hand a little as he took it, and at the second interval he got up and left the box. Suddenly, I realized what I had done. I had betrayed myself utterly, and in writing too! There was no telling how the Pole would react, but I knew that if Misha found out he wouldn't hesitate to denounce me. The interval seemed very long, and the lights were dimming when the major returned, carrying a huge bunch of lilac. As he gave me the flowers, he whispered, 'Thank you, Comrade.'

'I am so sorry,' he said to Misha when the ballet was over, 'I had been looking forward to spending the rest of the evening with you and your charming wife, but I've just heard that my colleagues have arranged a meeting at the hotel and I shall have to go straight back. So unfortunate, perhaps some other time . . . '

Misha was furious and grumbled all the way home.

'What an odd character! One minute he's all over you and the next he can't wait to get away!'

'But you heard what he said – he has a meeting.'

'Rubbish! I don't believe a word of it!'

So ended my first mission, with a bunch of lilac and a bad conscience. But General Sudoplatov seemed perfectly satisfied with my report.

'It confirms our opinions precisely. You say here that the Germans were praising and admiring everything, and that the Poles were not afraid to criticize. Exactly! The Germans are very reliable people, easily led. But with the Poles you can never be quite sure; they're too emotional altogether.'

I didn't say which attitude I had found more interesting.

'Now,' continued Sudoplatov, 'I'd like you to meet one of our most efficient female agents.' He pressed a button on the intercom. 'Send Captain Tamara Nikolaievna Ivanova to my office.'

She was a thin woman in her late thirties with cold blue eyes in a hard face. Her hair was scraped straight back and her uniform skirt was half-way to her ankles. I tried to pull mine down over my knees but she noticed at once that I had shortened it quite considerably. We really had nothing to say to each other.

'You may speak German together,' Sudoplatov beamed. 'Tamara Nikolaievna works in the Austrian department.'

Timidly, I murmured something about having a lot to learn.

'We all have,' Comrade Ivanova snapped, 'and we are still learning!'

Luckily she was called to the telephone. She swung out of the room with the energetic strides of an idealist.

'What did you think of her?' asked the general when we were alone again. I racked my brains for something kind to say.

'Her German is very good. Quite excellent.'

'Yes, and she speaks French, too. She's one of our mainstays, absolutely wedded to the office. A wonderful woman. I brought her in to show you, Jelena Kirilovna, the gap that we hope you will fill. There are some assignments for which Comrade Ivanova is quite unsuited. And now, may I have the pleasure of taking you out to lunch?'

CHAPTER THIRTEEN

Viennese Waltz

In the summer of 1950 I was enrolled for a six-month course at the Police College. I wore the black police uniform just like the other students, and none of them knew that I was a member of the State Security Service. I never learnt very much about them, either, apart from Natasha, a lively girl with whom I soon became friendly. One day there was an argument in class about whether it was ideologically sound to listen to the 'Voice of America' radio station.

'It's as bad as collaborating with the enemy!' one student said earnestly.

'No it's not! The music is fantastic; that's all I have it for.'

'And between the music programmes there's nothing but propaganda against the Soviet Union.'

'How do you know,' Natasha said, 'if you never listen to it?'

The earnest student blushed. 'Well, you know, one sometimes hears bits by accident.'

'At two o'clock in the morning?' Natasha grinned. 'Come off it! Just tell us what wavelength it's on!'

After that the latest American pop songs were constantly being sung and whistled around the police college.

Natasha often spent the evening with me in the flat, listening to Voice of America. Once, to my consternation, General Sudoplatov and Misha called in the middle of a jazz session. I quickly turned the radio off and waited for a scolding. But the general only switched it on again and began dancing with me.

'Who is that girl?' he asked.

'She's a student at the Police College – Home Office Prison Division.'

'Don't tell her who I am. It would spoil the party.'

I realized that he and Misha were a little drunk. Natasha and I weren't strictly sober either; we had been enjoying a vodka or two with the music. The men had brought champagne with them and we went on drinking and dancing until the small hours. I felt that, of us all, Sudoplatov was the one who really should have known better, but it was he who egged us on. Later, Natasha took over as ringleader.

'It's getting awfully hot in here!' she giggled. 'Let's take our clothes off!'

One by one, as we gyrated, our garments dropped on the floor. It was long before 'striptease' became a fashionable entertainment; we were, for once, a step ahead of the Americans.

*

I woke up with a splitting headache. Misha was beside me in the bed, and on the floor, stark naked, the general lay on his back, snoring peacefully. Natasha was curled up beside him with her head resting on his arm. Quietly, I drew blankets over the two men and shook Natasha awake.

'Come on. Let's get out of here!'

She groaned as she sat up. 'Who on earth is that?'

'He's a general in the Secret Service.'

'Oh my God!'

We flung our clothes on and went to the college. After work we hurried back to clean up the mess, and found it had all been done. The glasses were washed, the empty bottles had disappeared, and on the table stood a vase of carnations and a bottle of perfume. A card was propped up against them: 'Many thanks for a lovely evening. Pavel Antonovitch and Misha.' The hard men of the KGB were human after all.

After two months' basic training at the Police College, there was a six-weeks' course in politics and civics. It consisted mainly of propaganda lectures against the West and warnings about the infiltration of American agents. I didn't enjoy it much, though I managed to get good marks at the end. But the next course, on forensic medicine, finished me altogether. We had to watch post-mortem examinations of real corpses. Every murder victim was shown to us – and although they weren't reported in Russian newspapers, Moscow had as many and as gruesome murders as any other city. I fainted every time. The end came when they brought in a body which had been found in the stadium. It had been lying in the sun for a few days, and the murderer had cut out the man's eyes. When I came to, I had a screaming fit. I spent three days in the hospital and afterwards I couldn't bear to be alone in the flat. Misha reported me sick and I spent a week with him and his mother and Alik, trying to forget that rotting, eyeless face.

Then General Sudoplatov sent for me and I had to explain my absence from the course.

'I'm sorry, comrade,' he said, 'but it is deliberate policy to toughen our agents. You mustn't allow yourself to be so squeamish! However,' he continued, smiling, 'you're in luck, we have another assignment for you.'

He introduced me to an elegant man dressed in the latest Western fashion.

'Colonel Mirkovski is chief of the Intelligence Branch in Vienna. You will assist him and another officer in recruiting a very important contact.'

I had an aunt who lived in Vienna. The city had a Western sector, like Berlin. Was this a chance to escape?

'Could I take Alik with me?' I asked as casually as I could. 'It would be such a treat for him.'

'Certainly not!' Sudoplatov snapped. 'Your son will stay in the Soviet Union where he belongs!'

They had thought of everything. After an angry pause, the general continued:

'You will go to Austria as a single woman. You will dress in such a way as to show the capitalist world that we have everything here. The cashier will let you have the necessary funds.'

Mirkovski had been looking at me through narrowed eyes.

'I think she should have her hair dyed lighter,' he observed. The two men considered the matter.

'Yes,' agreed Sudoplatov, without asking my opinion. 'Go to the Intourist Hotel; they have Western hairdressers there.' He seemed quite unaware of any ironies.

Then he took a photograph from a file on his desk and handed it to me.

'This is the man we are interested in. His name is Hochstätter. He's a member of the Austrian communist party and manager of the passport office in a Vienna suburb. We want him to provide us with the following: Austrian identity cards, stamped and signed but otherwise blank, of course; an official stamp for the photographs; photocopies of the records of missing people. Is that clear?'

'But if he's a communist,' I said, 'why doesn't Colonel Mirkovski simply ask him for them?'

They both looked at me as if I had said something very stupid.

'For one thing,' the general said, 'Comrade Mirkovski must be as inconspicuous as possible in Vienna. For another, unlike our comrades in the East German Republic, we have no authority in Austria. And finally, Herr Hochstätter is a civil servant; we don't know how far his co-operation will extend. That is what you have to find out, Comrade Pushkova.'

*

The other KGB officer in the party was Major Okunin. He and I had to do a fortnight's course at the Railways Centre in order to be convincing members of a group of engineers going to Austria to buy machinery. We travelled in the black uniform of railway officers. Colonel Mirkovski met us at the airport, and during the official greetings I overheard someone say, 'Well, I'll be damned! I never knew the Russians had women who looked like that!'

Mirkovski smiled down at me. 'He's right, you know. The blonde hair suits you very well. If you're as efficient as you're beautiful, we can all congratulate ourselves.'

The first few days, negotiating the purchases, were boring beyond belief. My role was that of interpreter to the engineers and I had to be present at every conference. At last the contract was signed and Herr Baumgartner, the manufacturer – and, incidentally, close friend of Herr Hochstätter – invited us to a party at his house.

This was the crux of the assignment. It had been foreseen that there would be such a party, and that Herr Hochstätter was almost certain to be invited. The rest was up to me. He was, indeed, introduced to me quite early on, but I was so fascinated by Frau Baumgartner that I paid hardly any attention. She was a supremely elegant woman; her hair was a far more delicate ash blonde than mine; and for the first time in many years I was enjoying a conversation about clothes and hairdressers and all the feminine preoccupations my life had so conspicuously lacked.

Major Okunin recalled me to my duties. I sought out Herr Hochstätter, and he attached himself to me for the rest of the evening. He raved about Moscow, the Bolshoi Theatre, Red Square, the Kremlin – though he had never been to Russia.

'It's the same for me,' I said. 'Vienna is at least as beautiful as Moscow, I know, but I've hardly seen anything of it. It's very difficult for a stranger . . . '

He picked up his cue as if we had rehearsed it. 'Would you allow me to show you round? There's nothing I'd like better, I assure you.'

We arranged to spend Sunday together.

*

Part of my KGB equipment was a flat crocodile leather case containing a pistol, a Minox camera, a miniature radio transmitter and a quantity of American and Austrian money. I dressed carefully for the date with Hochstätter, in navy blue and white, and it seemed to me that the leather case spoiled the whole effect. There was nothing in it that I would need that day anyway, so I left it in the wardrobe and took instead a white handbag. Okunin was waiting in the foyer.

'All you need is a bunch of flowers,' he said unkindly, 'and we could be on our way to the registry office!'

I was furious that he insisted on coming with us; we had argued about it half the night. To spite him, I insisted on visiting every church and climbing to the top of every tower. Wherever we went, Okunin sweated after us; anyone would have thought he was trying to sabotage the assignment. Hochstätter did his best to entertain us both. We were sitting at a pavement café and he was telling us some longwinded political story, when Okunin suddenly interrupted.

'Where is your little case?' he asked me in Russian.

'I left it at the hotel. It didn't go with my dress.'

'But you took the things out of it?'

'Why, no. I had no need to carry all that stuff around.'

He jumped to his feet, white-faced. 'We must go back to the hotel at once!'

Herr Hochstätter came with us and we all rushed up to my room. Sure enough, the case had gone. Okunin went off to find the manager and I burst into tears. Hochstätter patted my hand; he seemed more cheerful than he had been all day.

'Please don't cry, my dear! I shall set the entire police force in motion for you. I have the power, you know.'

He probably had. This seemed a wonderful chance. I wiped my eyes and faced him squarely.

'We can't involve the police. I'll explain later. But you could help me in another way.'

'How? Just tell me!'

'Comrade Hochstätter, I have a confession to make. The major and I are members of the KGB.'

'Really? Is that really true?' His chubby face glowed with excitement. 'You are a genuine Secret Service agent for the Soviet Union!'

'We're here to protect the railway engineers, you see. And now that I've lost my little case, Central Office will never forgive me!'

'Oh, my dear, I do see that! You probably had some secret things in it?'

'A miniature radio transmitter,' I whispered, 'and a mini camera.'

He was so overawed that he could only repeat what I was saying. 'A miniature radio transmitter! Oh, if only I could help you!'

'But you can help me, Comrade Hochstätter! If you were to do me a certain favour, Central Office would probably over-look my mistake.'

He squeezed my hand and gazed into my eyes. I took a deep breath and recited the list of requirements the general had given me. Whenever I paused, Hochstätter prompted me, and I began to wonder if he was pulling my leg. But no, he was completely serious.

'Comrade, I am a true communist and for me there is only

102

one fatherland, the land of the working people. I am honoured to help the Soviet Union, and helping you personally is a particular pleasure!'

I threw my arms round his neck and kissed him, and he responded eagerly.

'Just tell me how, when, where.'

'Comrade Mirkovski will handle all that.'

'What! Is he a secret agent, too?'

I nodded, disengaged myself, and got a bottle of vodka from the cupboard.

'Nasdarovie, and thank you, comrade.'

We had had several vodkas by the time Major Okunin came back. He reported glumly that nothing had been found, and said we must hurry to Colonel Mirkovski's house, where we were expected for dinner.

'Fool!' he muttered to me on the way, 'vodka isn't the right consolation at a time like this. I advise you to own up to the colonel as soon as you can.'

'Don't worry! I intend to.'

I told Mirkovski as soon as we arrived that Herr Hochstätter had agreed to let us have the documents, and added sheepishly that I had lost my case.

'Oh – that!' Mirkovski said, 'I wondered how soon you would miss it.' He fetched it from the next room. 'I looked in to see you this morning but you had just left. Your room was being cleaned and I could see the case in the open cupboard, so I took charge of it just to be on the safe side. You're supposed to keep it with you all the time, you know.'

The rest of the evening was cheerful enough, but when I got to bed I couldn't sleep. Aunt Margaret lived only a few blocks away; surely it could do no harm just to see her before I went back to Moscow. In the end I couldn't resist it; I got up and dressed and crept out of the hotel. It was a quarter to one when I reached her house in a quiet residential street. I rang the doorbell for ages, but no one came. At last a window on the ground floor shot up and a cross voice asked what all the noise was about.

'I'm so sorry to disturb you. I am looking for Frau Withold.'

'She's not here; she's away on holiday. Don't you realize what the time is?'

Disappointment and homesickness swept over me as I retraced my steps. It had never occurred to me that she might not be there, when I wanted to see her so badly. A cruising taxi stopped at the kerb.

'Can I take you anywhere, lady?' I got in gratefully.

'Where to?' Where indeed? I couldn't bear the thought of going straight back to the hotel.

'Is there anywhere I could have a drink?'

The taxi driver looked a bit doubtful. 'There's not much open at this time of night. Would the Casino Oriental do?'

'I expect so.'

CHAPTER FOURTEEN

In the Line of Duty

It wouldn't really do at all; I could see that at a glance. I was hesitating in front of the swing doors when a firm hand grabbed my arm.

'Hello, darling, come on in!'

I couldn't resist without making a scene, which we had been taught never to do. My captor steered me through the dimly-lit bar and sat me at a small table.

'I'm Charlie,' he announced. 'What are you drinking?' Suddenly I wanted a drink very badly indeed, and asked for a whisky. I sat primly upright on my chair while Charlie tried to climb all over me. The Police College had taught me a few useful tricks, and I soon realized I had nothing to fear from him. He was just gloriously drunk.

Three half-naked girls were belly-dancing at the far end of the room, and when their show was over, the lights went up in the bar. I was amazed to find it was crowded with Americans, Englishmen, Frenchmen and Russians, each with a girl in attendance. Charlie turned out to be rather good looking in a crewcut, American way. He looked at me and whistled.

'Just let me finish my drink and go!' I begged him.

'No way! Stay with me, honey, and I promise to behave myself.'

'Then can I just make a telephone call?'

Charlie insisted on coming with me. I rang Okunin and told him where I was. He sounded furious. When I put the receiver down, Charlie was goggle-eyed.

105

'What language was that?'

'Russian.'

'Are you a refugee?'

'No, I'm an engineer with the Soviet Railways Ministry and my boss is coming to collect me.'

'Oh boy! We must have some champagne on that!'

He was really unstoppable. He gave me a visiting card – 'Charles Rudford, First Lieutenant, US Army' with his address and telephone number in Vienna on the back. He wanted to know everything about life in Russia. I repeated some of the platitudes from our civics course, constantly looking over his shoulder for Okunin.

At last he arrived and I stood up in relief. 'It's been very nice meeting you, Mr Rudford, but we must go now.'

'What's that?' exclaimed Okunin, drawing up a chair. 'The night is young. What shall we have to drink?'

We were there till dawn, and afterwards Okunin said: 'You did that very well indeed.'

'What do you mean? Charlie is completely harmless, surely you could see that!'

'There's no such thing as a harmless American.'

'If you want to work on Charlie I'll have nothing to do with it.'

'We'll see.'

*

When we flew back to Moscow, I had eight suitcases full of Western fabrics and clothes, and Okunin had a sealed package of Austrian official documents provided by Hochstätter.

'He sent his love,' Okunin said, 'and was sorry you were always too busy to see him. Charlie sent his love too. I promised you would get in touch.'

'Oh, go to hell.'

Okunin chuckled, and put the package in his briefcase.

'You'll learn,' he said.

Soon after I had sent in my report, I was called to Central Office. I missed a train and was late; punctuality was never my strong point and I felt more nervous than ever as I hurried through the corridors of the Lubianka to the Minister's room. Abakumov got up as I entered and made my apologies. General

Sudoplatov was standing at the window with a colonel I didn't know, and Okunin, to my annoyance, was there as well.

Abakumov turned to the general. 'The Underground is a very unreliable means of transport. See that Comrade Push-kova is issued with a car and chauffeur immediately.' He didn't appear to be joking.

He embraced me on both cheeks in the Russian manner and congratulated me on my performance in Vienna. Was this a joke too? I looked uneasily at Sudoplatov, but he nodded and smiled.

'Yes. Major Okunin has given us a detailed report. Not only did you recruit Hochstätter; you made a valuable contact with an American officer.'

'But it wasn't deliberate. He picked me up in a bar!'

'Exactly! Sometimes it takes us years to set up such a chance meeting, and you managed it in a few days.'

'Hours!' corrected Okunin proudly. The strange colonel looked me over with knowing eyes.

'She is precisely the magnet we need to attract men.' His manner infuriated me. 'I didn't go to Vienna to attract men, but to work!' I snapped at him, and everybody laughed.

'Bravo!' said Abakumov, 'that's what I call discipline! This is Colonel Shalatov of 8th Division, he will accompany you on your next assignment. General Sudoplatov will tell you about it.'

The Minister dismissed us, and we all went along to the general's office. Colonel Shalatov, it seemed, was particularly interested in my acquaintance with the American lieutenant, as it was his job to infiltrate Soviet agents among the armed forces of the West.

'Charlie Rudford wouldn't be any use to you!'

'That is for us to decide.'

The plan was that I should be employed for a few months at the Soviet Embassy in Vienna. I would have my own flat, and I would get in touch with Charlie.

'Very soon,' Shalatov continued, 'you will fall passionately in love with him.'

'Oh yes?' I hated the man more and more.

'You will invite him to your flat . . . '

'And go to bed with him, I suppose!'

'Of course.'

'And under the bed,' I was being sarcastic now, 'there will be a tape recorder.'

'Exactly.' Shalatov was perfectly serious. 'We will play the tape back to him, and if that isn't enough, we'll show him a few photographs.'

'What photographs?'

'There will be a camera hidden in your flat.'

'Taking pictures of him and me in bed?'

'Yes.'

'And I'll be in the pictures as well?'

'Naturally. There wouldn't be much point in them otherwise, would there?'

Okunin snorted with laughter. Seeing my outraged expression, Shalatov started laughing too, and soon all three men were roaring and slapping their thighs with mirth. I couldn't bear it. Rage and disgust took hold of me completely; I crossed the room and hit Colonel Shalatov hard in the face.

There was a shocked silence. Then General Sudoplatov quietly said: 'Get out!' I waited in the ante-room, and presently Okunin came out. He was shaking his head dazedly.

'It's unbelievable,' he said, 'just unbelievable!' I fell into a chair and burst into tears.

Okunin put a packet of cigarettes on the table. 'You are not to leave this room,' he said. 'That's an order!' Then he went back into the office.

I sat smoking one cigarette after another. For a long time I could hear the murmur of voices, then a door slammed and all was quiet. Lunchtime came and went. It began to get dark. There was no sound except my own breathing. Somewhere, a clock struck ten.

At eleven, Okunin appeared again.

'Your car is waiting downstairs, Comrade.'

'What is going to happen to me?' I asked him. He shrugged.

The next ten days were nerve-racking. I expected hourly to be arrested, but instead nothing happened at all. No one was available when I telephoned, nobody came near me. I lived like a hermit in the middle of the teeming city. I fetched Alik; he was company of a sort, and my days followed his nursery

routine. I took to going to church. There at least were people
I need not fear.

One evening I went round to Misha's place, pretending I
needed more nappies for Alik. He was there, but he wasn't
very pleased to see me.

'Won't you help me?' I begged him, 'or at least come and
talk to me! What am I supposed to do?'

'Just wait. And if I were you, I wouldn't go to church so
much. It doesn't look right for a KGB officer.'

So I was being watched! Misha didn't try to detain me, and
I went miserably home.

*

When the telephone finally rang I jumped as if a bomb had
gone off. It was General Sudoplatov.

'Comrade Pushkova? I just wanted to make sure you were
at home. Would it be convenient if I came to see you in about
half an hour?'

Precisely half an hour later the doorbell rang. The general
strode into the flat as if he owned it and started playing with
Alik. I made tea to cover my embarrassment, but my hand
trembled as I poured it.

'There's no need to be frightened of me, girl. We're all
human!'

He was in civilian clothes, perfectly relaxed; he lit a cigarette
and stretched out comfortably in his chair.

'But I have to talk to you about your conduct in my office.
A lieutenant on duty slapping the face of a colonel. I've never
heard anything like it!'

'I am very, very sorry, Comrade General.'

'So you should be! You are also very lucky. Colonel Shalatov
reported the incident to the Minister, but Comrade Abakumov
seems to have a soft spot for you. He was even impressed that
you defended your virtue so passionately.'

The general's mouth twitched; for an awful moment I
thought he was going to start laughing again. Then he went on:

'Anyway, the whole thing is to be forgiven and forgotten,
provided you behave responsibly in future and accept the
orders you are given.'

'Comrade General, I implore you. I'll never be able to carry out an assignment like the one with the American!'

'Rubbish!' Sudoplatov said comfortably. 'You're young. You'll learn.'

I was overwrought after the ten days of fear and tension, and I began to cry. The general got up and took me by the shoulders.

'Calm down, girl. You needn't do the job in Vienna. If I sent you there now the whole thing would go wrong anyway. All assignments must be undertaken voluntarily. That's one of our strictest principles!'

In the evening Misha called, quite his old friendly self.

'So everything is all right again. Well done, love.'

His cheerfulness infuriated me. 'No thanks to you! You didn't do a thing.'

'That's what you think. I've been to the general's office every day.'

I thumped the table with my fist. 'But it was here, here that I wanted you!'

'I couldn't, Lenotchka. You were in disgrace. I'd only have got myself in trouble too. Anyway, forget it. I've got good news. We're going together on the next assignment!'

'Where to?'

'Vladivostok.'

He told me about a railway wagon loaded with submarine parts that had vanished without trace on the way east. He was to pose as a naval engineer officer and try to find out what had happened to it.

'And what about me?'

'Oh, you'll just be my loving wife, keeping your eyes and ears open of course. It will be a holiday for you. But before we go you must mug up a little on ranks, naval jargon and so on, so that you make a convincing N.O.'s wife.'

It sounded rather fun. We boarded a plane on 12 November in the highest spirits. I had done my navy homework; and I had also, on the general's instructions, put in an official application for membership of the communist party. One couldn't be a good citizen anywhere, it seemed, without a membership book.

In Vladivostok we stayed with Captain Kandelka and his wife. Misha was busy and I had a lot of time on my hands.

Anela Petrovna Kandelka came from the Baltic States and her mother tongue was German; we soon became close friends. One day we were out shopping together when a man's voice interrupted us.

'This is too good to be true! Two German women on the outer fringes of Asia. I could hardly believe my ears when I heard you talking!'

I swung round. 'I'm afraid you're mistaken; we're both Russian.'

'But that's extraordinary. I could have sworn I could pin-point the exact districts you came from. Oh well,' he sighed, 'won't you at least join me in a glass of tea?'

His child-like blue eyes became quite misty when we refused, and he pointed to a café across the street. 'I am there every afternoon at five. It would be such a pleasure to talk to you some time.'

The very next day I made an excuse to our hostess and slipped out to meet Herr Johannsen. He had seemed so lost and pathetic; and I, too, was dying to talk to a fellow-countryman. He greeted me with amazed delight and immediately told me all about himself. It was a familiar story. An engineer by profession, he had been taken prisoner-of-war in 1942, served five years in a labour camp, and had then been released on condition he stayed in the Soviet Union. He worked in the submarine depot at Vladivostok.

'It's not such a bad life, I suppose,' he ended, 'but all I really want is to get back to Germany.'

'I can understand that!'

Johannsen was gazing into the distance. 'There is a way of getting out illegally.'

'Then why don't you go?'

'It takes a long time to save the money. And I'm not sure. There's something funny about it. Two of my friends left that way and promised to send postcards, but I've never heard from either of them.'

'Tell me how they went.'

Johannsen leant a little closer across the table.

'There's a man here, a captain in the Merchant Navy, who will take refugees abroad. If they've got money, that is.'

'Where does he take them?'

111

'Oh, to Japan, Australia, America. It depends where he's going at the time.'

'What does it cost?'

' I believe he usually charges 10,000 roubles. And every now and then he betrays one of them to the KGB, just to safeguard himself. I expect you know who the KGB are?'

'Yes. What is his name?'

'Captain Dashkin.'

I told Misha all about it when I got back, but he wasn't very impressed.

'There are stories like that in every camp and prison in the country. This is a restricted military area; it would be impossible to smuggle anyone out. I bet you the mysterious Captain Dashkin doesn't even exist!' He laughed. 'I've got news for you, too – we're going home. That missing truck has been found in a siding at Chabarovsk. There wasn't any sabotage, it was just forgotten!'

At dinner that night I asked our host if he knew a Captain Dashkin.

'Yes, of course I do. Why?'

I gave Misha a triumphant glance and repeated what Johannsen had told me. Anela was indignant.

'That's impossible, he's such a nice man!' But her husband looked quite serious.

'I don't know. I've been wondering for some time how he could afford his life-style on a merchant navy salary. There might be something in it.'

Misha was really interested at last, and next day he went to see the local KGB officer, Colonel Voronin.

'It's true,' he said when he came back. 'Dashkin has surrendered one or two stowaways. I think we should look into it.'

We discussed what to do. Herr Johannsen was such a trusting soul, I didn't like the idea of using him as stoolpigeon.

'All right then,' Misha said at last. 'The only other way is to tell him the truth. Explain who you are and promise him he can go home legally if he helps us to get Dashkin.'

It was a delicate piece of negotiation; eventually Johannsen gave me the captain's telephone number and the code message 'I want to go on a trip.'

I made the call from the KGB office in the presence of

Misha and Voronin and with a tape recorder wired to the telephone.

'Who are you?' Dashkin asked, after I had repeated the message twice in a thick accent.

'My name is Helga and I am German.'

'How old are you, and what colour is your hair?'

I told him.

'I shall be at the café Metro tomorrow afternoon at five. I'll be reading the *Isvestiya*.' He put the receiver down and I turned to the two men.

'What do you say now?'

Voronin's face was grave. 'I would never have believed it of him!'

'Ah,' said Misha, 'you need General Sudoplatov's motto – Think the worst of everybody, always.'

CHAPTER FIFTEEN

The Gentle German

At five o'clock next day I met Dashkin at the café Metro; his newspaper was spread all over the table. I had a mini tape-recorder concealed in my bag. He looked me up and down, but left me to start the conversation.

'I telephoned you about the trip.'

'Oh yes – where do you want to go?'

'It doesn't much matter. America would be nice.'

'Tell me everything about yourself.'

I told him the story Misha and I had rehearsed; that I was working in Vladivostok with a group of specialist engineers from Germany, and that a colleague wanted to come with me.

Dashkin seemed satisfied. 'There are two tickets left. The price for the engineer is 10,000 roubles. But for you,' he undressed me with his eyes, 'it is only 8,000. We sail at four o'clock on Friday morning for San Francisco. Meet me at eleven on Thursday night, pier no. 7. Pay in cash, when you are on board.'

On Thursday night, Colonel Voronin gave us each the money for our fare, in used notes. Then he took two fountain pens out of his pocket and handed one to me.

'You know how this thing works?' I nodded and put it in my bag. Johannsen looked completely baffled. Voronin aimed the pen at him like a pistol.

'If I now pressed the metal clip, you would get a squirt of gas in your face that would put you out for at least a couple of hours. Okay?' He gave Johannsen the pen. 'Only use it in an emergency.'

'Good luck!' Misha whispered, 'and don't worry. We'll be watching the ship all the time, and we'll come aboard with the Customs officers an hour before you sail. Scream if there's any trouble.'

At pier no. 7 Dashkin dressed us up in white coats and gave us a bucket and a first aid box to carry.

'Just till we get on board,' he said, and strode off into the dark. We hurried after him. He led us to a cabin on the lower deck where a young man was sitting on a bench.

'Wait here.'

The young man was staring at the floor and nervously cracking his finger joints. No one spoke. Presently Dashkin reappeared and told me to go with him. He led me through the darkened ship to a door marked 'Sick Bay'.

'Our doctor will give you a check-up now.'

An almond-eyed young woman in a white coat looked at my tonsils, pulled down my eyelids and felt the glands in my neck.

'Very good.'

'Well then, shall we settle the financial side?'

I counted out 8,000 roubles. Dashkin put the money in his pocket.

'Have you got any valuables on you? You know smuggling is not allowed.'

I shook my head, but he wasn't satisfied.

'Do you mind if I look in your bag?'

I held my breath as he riffled through it, but he took no notice of the fountain pen.

The sick bay was a brightly-lit, white-painted room with a row of lockers reaching from floor to ceiling along one side.

'During the Customs check,' Dashkin continued, 'you will hide in one of these lockers. The doors can be fastened from the inside. No Customs officer has ever asked to look in them!' He giggled and nudged me with loathsome familiarity; then, glancing at the doctor, he took me back to the cabin and led Johannsen away.

The strange young man was still cracking his finger joints, and after a time it got on my nerves.

'Would you mind not doing that!'

'I'm terribly sorry, it's a stupid habit. Are you going abroad, too?'

I nodded, and he began to talk as if nothing would ever stop him. He was from the Baltic States. his parents were dead and he was going to relatives in America. He had literally starved in order to save the money.

'The real price is 10,000 roubles and I couldn't get beyond 7,000, but Captain Dashkin agreed to take me all the same. Wasn't that generous of him?'

Just then, the captain and Johannsen came back and Dashkin nodded at the young man.

'Your turn now.' They went out together.

Johannsen and I sat and waited. The time passed very slowly. I was thirsty and tired and began to wish our paths had never crossed. The young man from the Baltic didn't come back; but at a quarter to three the captain opened the door and called, 'Come with me, quickly!' He hurried us along to the sick bay, which was now only dimly lit by one small bulb above the door. I noticed a strong smell of ether.

'When a red light comes on,' Dashkin said tersely, 'get in the lockers. Don't talk and don't smoke.' He went out and locked the door after him.

It was all very different from the cheerful room I had seen earlier, and the smell of ether made me feel sick. I sat down on the floor, shivering with tension and nausea.

'I expect there are some blankets somewhere,' Johannsen whispered, and he began looking in the lockers. One of the doors was jammed. He found a pair of scissors and tried to prise it open.

'Come and hold a match for me, will you?'

I got up and lit a match and held it while Johannsen forced the door. Inside the locker the young man from the Baltic was hanging upside down, naked, with two long cuts gaping on either side of his neck. His dead eyes stared straight into mine; and under his head stood a bowl filled to the brim with blood.

There was a split-second before my mind registered what I was looking at, and then I dropped the match and started screaming at the top of my voice. There were running foot-

116

steps outside, the door was smashed open, and I flung myself, still screaming, into Misha's arms.

*

Anela Petrovna put me to bed and stayed with me until I fell into an uneasy sleep. At lunchtime next day, Misha came up to see me.

'Congratulations!' he said. 'Voronin is delighted and sends you his regards. It was much worse than we could have imagined. Dashkin was a mass murderer; he must have been doing it for years. Every time his ship sailed he took two or three refugees, at about 10,000 roubles a time, and under pretence of that medical examination he and his girlfriend anaesthetized them and cut their arteries.'

'Then why didn't he kill us?'

Misha smiled. 'Well, he had other plans for you, my sweet, and I suppose he thought it would be more amusing if Johannsen was alive to watch. You're both very lucky.'

*

Herr Johannsen travelled to Moscow with us at the government's expense, and I was happy to think that he would soon be back in Germany. Misha and I were summoned to a celebration at Central Office, where we were hailed as 'The Heroes of Vladivostok'. Champagne and vodka were flowing freely; and I had to avoid catching Misha's eye while General Sudoplatov made a speech praising our courage and initiative. We were each decorated with the Red Banner medal; I was promoted to First Lieutenant and officially accepted into the communist party. As I received my membership book and bowed my head for the medal ribbon, I couldn't help wondering whether all heroes were as frightened and unheroic as I had been.

Johannsen had promised to say goodbye to us before he left, and three weeks later I began to wonder why he hadn't bothered. It turned out that he was still in Russia, and I got permission to visit him. He was lodged in one of the KGB 'guest houses' just outside the city, and he seemed overjoyed to see me.

'It's very comfortable here – but I feel like a prisoner. Nobody will tell me anything, but I'm pretty sure nothing has been done about my exit permit.'

'What makes you say that?'

'Well, you see, almost every day somebody comes and talks to me about the advantages of working for the Secret Service.'

'Don't do it, Herr Johannsen!'

I hurried back to General Sudoplatov and reminded him of our promise, and grudgingly he agreed to let Johannsen go. But he never did. Months later, I happened to meet the gentle German again. He told me he was working in the Naval Ministry.

'Oh! However did they make you?'

'Nobody made me. I decided it was the best thing. It was all quite voluntary.'

But nothing would make him look me in the eye.

*

The next assignment for Misha and me was the New Year's Eve fancy dress ball at the Kremlin. It was a glittering occasion; all the highest in the land were there – the élite of the new classless society – as well as the distinguished foreign visitors with whom we had been told to mingle. I had decided fancy dress would be unsuitable as I was there on duty, and I was wearing one of the grandest dresses from my Viennese collection. Misha, who in real life had just been promoted to Lieutenant-Colonel, was in uniform as Commander Tshernikov of the Soviet Navy.

Promptly at midnight, as the bells rang out in Red Square, Comrade Stalin made his entrance in the white and gold uniform of Generalissimo of the Armed Forces. In the silence of the great hall, his husky voice proposed the toast: 'To our Soviet Fatherland.' And like a litany his guests replied: 'To our genius, leader and teacher, to our beloved Comrade Stalin. Hurrah! Hurrah! Hurrah!' Glasses were emptied; there was a general hand-shaking and embracing, and Stalin was gone again as suddenly as he had come. I thought of the millions all over Russia who would be drinking his health at that moment, hoping for a better year, for some relaxation of the terror, for more bread, more meat, more milk, and even for a new pair of shoes.

Misha didn't care for dancing and was much happier propping up the bar. We were sipping champagne together and I was berating him for his stuffiness, when a handsome young man dressed as a Don Cossack stopped in front of me and clicked his heels.

'May I?'

'Oh, please do – take her away,' Misha said carelessly. 'All she wants to do is dance!'

The young man was an excellent dancer, and an amusing companion, too. He told me his name was Semyon Beria and that he was an engineer. After several dances we went back to find Misha, who was at the bar exactly where we had left him. Introductions were made.

'Beria?' Misha gasped, 'then you must be the son of . . . '

'That's right,' said Semyon cheerfully. 'He's my old man.'

All of a sudden Misha wanted to dance.

'Good grief,' he muttered as we circled the floor, 'you really have caught a big fish! Didn't you realize . . . ?'

I hadn't, of course. But now it struck me that this charming young man's father, Minister of the Interior, second only to Stalin himself, was just the ally I needed in my fight for Andrei's release. I smiled at Semyon as our eyes met and Misha released me.

'Behave yourself!' he muttered and left us together.

We danced every dance for the rest of the night, and had our share of caviare and champagne in the intervals. When the ball was over, Semyon loaded me into his black ZIM car and his chauffeur drove us away. We were both rather drunk; I sank against his chest and fell asleep.

*

I woke up in a huge pink four-poster bed. The whole room was a symphony in pink and blue, like a rather vulgar film set. It was broad daylight and the light was painful. Presently Semyon Beria knocked and came in; dressed in a dark suit, I hardly recognized him. He seemed unnaturally sprightly considering the night we had had.

'Did you sleep well?'

'Yes, I think so. Is your father here?'

'I really don't know. He won't bother us if he is.'

119

It was going to be more difficult than I'd imagined. I didn't know how to explain to this self-confident young man that it was only his father I was interested in.

The house was enormous, furnished and decorated in rococo style with money rather than taste. A liveried man-servant gave us a meal of roast pheasant and salad, and then Semyon saw me into the car.

'You must come riding with me some time. We have a stableful of horses.'

'Are you a communist?' I asked him.

'Why yes, of course, naturally.'

As the car traversed the rolling parklands of the Beria estate, and passed through guards and watch-towers on to the public road, I thought of Semyon's father, the revolutionary in leather jacket and balloon cap, fighting, when he was Semyon's age, the bloody war against privilege.

CHAPTER SIXTEEN

A Birthday Present

Then there was the Paris affair. Misha and I were told to go there and 'eliminate' two men who were proving an embarrassment, using fountain pens with lethal charges. I was appalled, and even Misha, who was much harder-bitten than I, protested that we were not killers.

'All right, then,' said the general, 'give me your reasons in writing for not wanting this assignment. Each of you separately.'

We did so – and a few days later, Misha was attacked by two thugs on his way home from work and left lying unconscious in the snow. As soon as I heard about it, I rushed to see him in hospital. His head was swathed in bandages.

'At least we won't have to go to Paris now!' he grinned. But he was wrong. Sudoplatov sent for me again. A stranger was standing in his office.

'We were all so sorry to hear of the accident to Comrade Tshernikov,' said the general blandly. 'But I would like you to meet Lieutenant-Colonel Gorniak; he has accepted the Paris assignment. If you will agree to accompany him, we are prepared to consider the possibility of having your husband moved to Moscow.' I knew then that I should have to go.

Gorniak was an ex-guerrilla leader and a ruthless and experienced agent. I felt completely out of my depth with him – but I was determined to save those two men if I could. As it turned out, I had a perfect opportunity. Gorniak needed some information from one of the victims – who was himself a KGB officer – and accepted an invitation to dine with him. As soon as he had gone, I too slipped out of the hotel and went to tell his friend why we were there. Within a few hours, both men had left the country; they were tracked as far as Copenhagen and after that even the KGB lost touch. Gorniak and I were recalled to Moscow under a cloud.

Misha was out of hospital by then and he came round at once to my flat.

'I hear the Paris mission was a failure. The general is furious – but perhaps you don't mind too much?'

I pulled the telephone plug out of the wall, as we always did when we wanted to talk privately in case the instrument had been bugged. Then I told him what I had done.

'Oh, Lenotchka, what frightful risks you take! But you seem to have got away with it; nobody seriously thinks the men were warned. Anyway– how lovely to have you back! I've missed you.'

'I've missed you too, Misha.'

We had a delightful evening together. Next morning I fetched Alik from his mother's flat and went on to the photographers to collect some snapshots I had taken on the boy's birthday.

'They have come out particularly well, Comrade Pushkova,' said the man in the shop. 'I have taken the liberty of enlarging one of them; let's say it is my birthday present to your son.'

He had even put it in a frame. I was very touched, and as soon as we got home I fetched hammer and nails to hang it on the wall above my bed.

The first nail disappeared straight into the wall. I tried again a little higher, and the same thing happened. Then I tapped carefully around the holes, and, sick with terror, began pulling off the wallpaper. Underneath was a square piece of cardboard covering an opening, and behind it, a microphone.

I snatched Alik up and rushed to Misha's flat. His mother was astonished to see us and I had to keep up some sort of demented conversation until Misha came home. All the time I was trying to remember exactly what I had said the previous evening; it was too much, whatever else. The only private place to talk was in the Underground. We sat on a bench in the lonely splendour of marble and crystal chandeliers, and I told Misha of my discovery.

'There's only one hope,' he said when I had finished. 'You must make a full confession. Don't mention the microphone, of course; it must look as though you've been driven to it by your conscience. And don't leave anything out; they'll check every smallest detail. Go back and do it now; I'll call you in the morning.'

The first thing I did when I got home was to replace the square of cardboard in front of the microphone and carefully stick back the wallpaper. Then I sat down to write my confession. It wasn't easy to make out a good case for myself, and I tore up draft after draft.

Misha didn't phone in the morning but he pushed a note under the door telling me to meet him again at Komsomolskaya station.

'I've checked everything,' he said. 'That bugging device is worked from the flat next door, and they've got it all on tape. The only thing I don't know is whether Central Office have already listened to our last conversation.' He broke off and looked at me miserably. 'Don't misunderstand me, love, but I've got to denounce you. Let me get my report in first, before your confession. Then, if they lock you up, at least I may be free to try and help you. If they get us both, there's no hope at all.' He stood up. 'We mustn't meet again. Don't deliver your story before eleven. Good luck, Lenotchka.' He walked quickly away without looking back.

I took my confession to the office just after eleven and then I collected Alik from Misha's flat. We might as well be together while we could. I took him to lunch in the best restaurant I knew, and afterwards to the Moscow State Circus. He was far too young to appreciate any of it; it was my gesture of defiance.

*

When we got home, the flat had been turned inside out. Everything from the cupboards and drawers was strewn over the floor. My jewellery had gone, my letters, personal papers and my pistol. But why hadn't they simply come to arrest me? Perhaps it was just a burglary, after all. Misha would know.

I picked up the telephone, but it was only connected to the guard on duty in the hall. It was the KGB, all right.

I had just finished putting Alik to bed when General Sudoplatov, Lieutenant-Colonel Gorniak, and that dreadful woman, Major Ivanova, came storming in. They suggested that we went next door for the interrogation.

'Don't worry – you'll hear your child if he cries!'

The neighbouring flat had the same layout as mine but it was furnished as an office, with a padded door, two telephones and a lot of technical equipment. The officer on duty cleared a space for us.

'Comrade Pushkova, who put you up to informing these men in Paris of our plans?'

'Nobody did. It was my own idea. I considered it a better solution than killing them.'

'Well then, who asked you to look for a better solution? You were sent to Paris to carry out specific orders. Now we shall be a laughing-stock all over France.'

'Comrade General, if you read one word about the affair in a newspaper, you can have me shot!'

'That is not within my province. You will be convicted according to the law. Now, tell us the whole story again from the beginning.'

It went on all night. In the morning they made me take Alik to a children's home, and then I was left alone as utterly as I had been after the face-slapping incident. But this time I was in much more serious trouble.

I was so certain of arrest that I even prepared a survival kit for Siberia: diced bread and onions dried over the stove; beans, sugar, and salt in linen bags; sewing needles and a pair of scissors. Late one night, in mid-February, came the long-awaited ring at the doorbell. I was ready for it; I gathered my necessities together and opened the door.

Semyon Beria stood there, a fur coat hanging from one shoulder, a fur cap perched at an angle on his dark curly hair. He saw the bag in my hand.

'Are you just off somewhere?'

'Perhaps . . . ' He walked past me into the flat.

'What's the matter with your telephone? I've been trying to ring you for over an hour.'

124

The guard next door would be listening eagerly to all this, I knew. I might as well tell him who my visitor was.

'There must be something wrong with the line, Semyon Larentiyovitch Beria, it happens all the time.' I spoke his name particularly clearly, and Semyon looked at me with a puzzled expression.

'You look pale! You're not ill, are you? Come on – change into something nice, we're going dancing!'

It was Soviet Forces Day, he reminded me, and there was a ball at Red Army house. I put on a dress that I had bought in Paris, but I didn't really expect to get down the stairs without a guard barring my way. Nothing happened; and there were no shocked faces at the party either, as there was no one there I knew. This was a different section of the privileged, mostly young Air Force officers with high ranks and many medals. One of them came up to Semyon and, after an arrogant appraisal of me, asked to be introduced.

'Certainly, my friend. Major-General Vassiliy Josephovitch Stalin: First Lieutenant Jelena Kirilovna Pushkova of the State Security Service.'

I might be due for court-martial and Siberia, but for the moment I was standing between the sons of the two most powerful men in Russia. It was too good an opportunity to miss. I gave Vassiliy an encouraging smile; he swept me on to the dance floor and monopolized me for the rest of the evening. But unfortunately he was in no mood for any serious conversation; he was drinking hard, and before long his behaviour was making us both conspicuous. Semyon had disappeared. I could see the looks Vassiliy was getting from his brother officers and realized it was up to me to do something.

'Vasya, I think I ought to go home now.'

When he heard that I had my own flat, he was only too eager to take me. I hoped the listener on the other side of the wall would be suitably impressed. But as we were putting on our coats in the foyer, a man in civilian clothes tapped me on the shoulder.

'Comrade Pushkova, will you please come with me.' He showed me the familiar red card.

'What's going on?' asked Vassiliy impatiently. 'Don't you know who I am?'

'Of course I do, Comrade General.'

'Well then – buzz off!' He seized my arm and hurried me to the car. The KGB officer got there first.

'Forgive me, Comrade General! Your companion is under arrest.'

'Well, I'll be damned!' The news seemed to sober him up a bit. 'Just let me talk to her first. I'll see she doesn't abscond. Where shall I take her, afterwards?'

'To the Lubianka, please, First Division.' The KGB man seemed almost grateful.

As soon as we were in the car I burst into tears.

'Oh hell!' said Vassiliy. 'We'd better go and see Comrade Serov.'

'Who's he?'

'He's Abakumov's deputy. He'll know what the problem is.'

There was another party going on in Serov's flat. Vassiliy asked to speak privately to his host and I was left, embarrassed, among the distinguished guests.

'Come and sit with us,' said a woman kindly. 'What a beautiful dress! You didn't buy that in Moscow, surely!'

Someone handed me a vodka. I had drunk far too much already and my eyes kept straying to the door where Vassiliy and Serov had disappeared. At last, Vassiliy came back and it was my turn. Serov was sitting in an armchair, smoking. He looked exactly like a kindly schoolmaster.

'Suppose you tell me all about it.'

I described the Paris assignment and told him that I had warned its victims. He listened in silence, only shaking his head now and then. When I had finished, he asked:

'Do you feel that you were right in acting the way you did?'

'From a humanitarian point of view, yes.'

'From a humanitarian point of view! How long have you been with the KGB?'

'Ten months.'

'And how old are you?'

'Twenty-three.'

'What training have you had?'

'I almost completed the Police College course.'

'You haven't been to Dzerzhinski Academy?'

'No.'

126

'And who sent you to Paris?'

'General Sudoplatov.'

Serov's colourless eyes looked me up and down. He ground his cigarette into the ashtray and exclaimed:

'Sudoplatov is an idiot.'

*

The upshot of it all was that, instead of being court-martialled, I was sent to do a course at Dzerzhinski Military and Diplomatic Faculty, beginning on 1 March, 1951. The students were all KGB officers, and I was the only woman. Our subjects were constitution studies, foreign relations, history and law. It was dry stuff; I found the difference between communist theory and Soviet practice quite inscrutable, and the many technical terms in the lectures taxed my knowledge of Russian to the limit. I quickly came to hate the Academy and to look around for an escape.

Early in May, a poster appeared on the students' notice board asking for volunteers to work in the Ural Mountains. Andrei's last known whereabouts had been a labour camp called Shabaresk, somewhere in the Urals. Perhaps I could kill two birds with one stone. I applied for a job and was accepted with alacrity; I was the only volunteer.

Sudoplatov was furious; and so was Misha, who behaved like a jealous husband.

'I don't have to take any notice of what you say,' I reminded him. 'It's Andrei I'm married to.'

'You'll live to regret it,' he promised darkly. 'You've no idea what life is like out there.'

CHAPTER SEVENTEEN

'That Dreadful Island'

I did regret it almost at once. I was sent to Kazan, capital of the Tartar Republic. An icy wind was blowing on the day I arrived there with Alik; the town was still covered with snow in the middle of May and the River Volga was frozen solid. Hungry, ill-dressed people queued outside the food shops all day long, and the lack of hygiene was frightening.

Lodgings had been arranged for me in the house of an old widow; the room smelt of sour milk, dried mushrooms and stale cigarette smoke. After one night, Alik and I were both covered in bug bites. I sent an urgent request to Misha for six rolls of wallpaper; then I scrubbed and disinfected the room and sprayed paraffin between the floorboards. No sooner was the room clean and comfortable that the widow wanted it for herself; I moved into her former room and went through the debugging operation all over again. Then that room was needed for the widow's daughter. When I had transformed the third and last room, the house was put up for sale.

I was offered a home with the widow's parents, but I had had enough of this game by now and I bought a house of my own in the neighbouring town of Zenelodolsk and employed a woman to look after Alik. My job was described as 'social and political care' of the foreign students at Kazan University and prisoners at Zenelodolsk labour camp. I was naturally more interested in the prisoners than in the students, and, under pretext of 'establishing contact', I questioned them closely about what other

128

camps they had been in and what other prisoners they knew. But none of them had ever heard of Andrei.

On a hill above the town I found the remains of a German military cemetery. It was utterly neglected; the wooden crosses had fallen over and cows grazed and trampled on the graves. As I tried to read some of the forgotten names, the place seemed to symbolize the hopelessness of my search.

*

Then the local Party secretary told me I was to act as guide to a delegation from East Germany that was coming to inspect the power station at Sverdlovsk and talk to the German students in the university.

'Comrade Secretary, whatever will they say when they see the military cemetery!'

There was just time to put it right. The visitors' sightseeing tour ended at the cemetery, which was enclosed by a new white fence. Inside, the mounds were covered in red gravel according to Russian custom and each had a freshly-painted nameboard. The German comrades walked among the rows of graves, reading the names and nodding to each other. One of them remarked: 'Fascist propaganda has always claimed that the dead are not honoured in the Soviet Union.'

'Ah,' smiled the Party secretary, 'that's another of those well-known capitalist lies!'

*

Shortly after this I was summoned back to Moscow. Major-General Miranov, Chief of Personnel, wanted to see me. I wondered what was wrong this time.

Nothing was wrong at all, and my past faults seemed quite forgiven and forgotten. Miranov had received a letter from the East German ambassador thanking him for a lunch party I had given for the delegates before they left Kazan. It was quite a simple affair, as no luxuries were obtainable, but I had done my best to provide an attractive setting – and made sure there was plenty of vodka.

'The Germans feel they have had a glimpse of the gracious living normal in private homes in the Urals,' said Miranov with a wry smile. 'This is exactly the sort of propaganda we want. I understand it was your idea to have the cemetery done up, too. Congratulations! I am very pleased with you, comrade!' He gave me a cash voucher for 2,000 roubles to cover the cost of the lunch.

'We shall be making more use of you in future as a guide for foreign visitors. You are to attend the Institute of Advanced Studies in Kazan; the course is part-time, it won't interfere with your work. And finally – the Minister would like to take you out to dinner. Be ready at eight o'clock.'

Abakumov looked greyer and unhealthier than ever, his eyes surrounded by blue shadows. He ate hardly anything.

'You look very pretty, my dear. Where did you get that dress?'

'In Paris.'

'Oh – you've been to Paris, have you?' Surely he must be pulling my leg!

'Comrade Minister, you sent me there yourself, remember?'

'I do indeed remember. You gave us all a great deal of trouble.'

'But you did nothing to help me!'

Abakumov's eyebrows shot up. 'If that were the case, you certainly wouldn't be sitting here now! No – I had to work very hard indeed to find a reason why you needn't be shot.'

'But it was Comrade Serov who . . .'

'Yes, it was he who pointed out that you were too inexperienced for such a mission. I was delighted to agree with him!'

He took my hand and stroked it. 'I am very glad that everything has turned out so well. You are too young and too pretty to die.'

As we left the restaurant, Abakumov looked at me keenly.

'You're not in any hurry, are you? I should like to talk to you about your husband.'

Instantly I was wide awake. 'Oh no, comrade, I'm in no hurry at all!'

'Then we'll go to my dacha.'

The dacha turned out to be just as sumptuous as Beria's country house. Abakumov showed me round with an almost child-like pride, and told me about his rose gardens and his servants and his two cooks who were on duty alternately all round the clock, ready to provide a meal at any time of day or night. Who for, I wondered; I had seldom met a man less interested in food!

Then he sat me down on a sofa and started telling me how lonely his life was; how hard, and sometimes cruel, the responsibilities of his high office; how much he longed for the love of a woman. I couldn't help feeling almost sorry for him as he gazed at me with his sad eyes.

'I am an old man, and my health isn't good. I won't demand of you what younger men would claim. All I want is sympathy, warmth, and perhaps a little affection. Do you understand me, my dear?' He seemed satisfied with my nod. 'And now, what was it you wanted to ask me, little one?'

I told him how I'd volunteered for the Urals in the hope that Andrei might be in a camp there, and how all my enquiries had drawn a blank.

'Good grief! Was that why you went? How could you be such a fool? Your husband's nowhere near the Urals.'

'So you do know where he is!'

'Of course. He's on Novaya Zemlya.'

'Oh no! Poor Andrei!'

Novaya Zemlya is an island off the north Siberian coast, not far from the Arctic Circle and 1,500 miles from Kazan.

'Please, Nikolai Alexandrovitch, get him out of there!'

'You overrate my powers, little one.'

'No I don't. You could have him moved if you wanted to.'

'I'll ring Comrade Varenzo first thing in the morning.'

For once, the Minister kept his word.

*

Marshal Varenzo was in charge of missile development; he received me at his headquarters just outside Moscow.

'So you are the wife of my old comrade-in-arms, Andrei Nikolaievitch. I wish I could do something for him, he was a first-rate commander. But I haven't much power where prisoners are concerned. I couldn't even save my own son-in-law when he was sentenced to death for sabotage. My daughter shot herself, you know.' He said it with something approaching pride, though his eyes were wet.

I was struck speechless; and Varenzo continued:

'First of all, we must get him off that dreadful island. Perhaps we could have him transferred to a missile test base as a specialist engineer, and then we could think about putting in a plea for clemency. It might work; you never know. And if Minister Abakumov would put in a word as well . . . But it would all take time.'

'Meanwhile, is there any chance of my being able to see him?'

He glanced at my uniform. 'Novaya Zemlya is restricted territory, but for you, as an officer with the State Security Service, it might be possible. Let's see.' He consulted a diary on his desk. 'Yes, a group of engineers is flying up there in October. Only for twenty-four hours, but you would have time to talk to him. I'll see if I can work it.'

*

I went back to Kazan and enrolled at the Institute of Advanced Studies. What with a full day-time job, and lectures every evening, time passed very quickly until mid-October when I was recalled to Moscow to prepare for the trip. Special clothes were needed for the Arctic winter; and in addition, I took two suitcases full of things for Andrei – woollens, cigarettes, chocolate, tinned food and fruit.

After a six-hour flight, the aircraft landed in a desert of snow. The outside temperature was forty-five degrees of frost; I could feel the cold bite into my legs as I started down the gangway. Someone hauled me back and made me put on long felt boots several sizes too large, and I staggered to the Nissen hut that served as a reception building. From there, dog-drawn sledges took us to the camp.

I was shown to a room in the administration block, and after unpacking and taking off the enormous boots, I went down to lunch. The dining hall was full of men; they stared as if I was a creature from another world. After lunch, the camp commandant came up to me, slightly embarrassed.

'If you don't mind, comrade, it would be better if you'd stay in your room. No one here has seen a woman for months – not to mention the prisoners. Your husband will be taken to you presently; you may have two hours with him.'

I went upstairs and stood by the window, waiting. Then it struck me that it was a mistake to be in uniform, and I got a dress out of my suitcase. I had just thrown my belt on to the bed when there was a knock on the door.

'Come in!'

The stranger who stood uncertainly in the doorway was wearing a dark quilted jacket, quilted trousers and thick boots. The number A1379 was stencilled on the right trouser leg. He was terribly thin and his shorn head balanced on a neck that seemed to consist only of tendons. I silently prayed that when Andrei came, he wouldn't look as bad as this.

The prisoner's adam's apple was jerking up and down. At last he managed to speak:

'My name is Andrei Nikolaievitch Sidrov.'

The voice at least was recognizable. I fought down my shock and horror and rushed to take him in my arms. Then I took off his boots and the filthy jackets and we sat down together on the bed. He was completely confused.

'Nobody told me you were coming . . . I would never have imagined . . . and the uniform . . . and that blonde hair. When I last saw you, at the trial, you looked so ill. And the child? It's dead, isn't it?'

I was half laughing and half crying. 'No, no, he's alive. You have a beautiful son!' I gave him Alik's latest photograph. Tears were pouring down Andrei's cheeks. I opened the suitcases and showed him the gifts I'd brought.

'Do they starve you, darling? You look so thin and ill!'

'No, not really. I've had a poor digestion ever since the Leningrad campaign. The food here is so greasy – because of the cold, you know – I can't manage it.'

'Ah, when you're free, I'll take you to a clinic.'

Andrei gave a forlorn smile. 'I have another eight years to go!'

'Not necessarily.' I told him about Varenzo and Abakumov and their plans for an appeal. He listened quietly.

'I'm not sure that I believe in all that. But never mind. I've seen you and our son is alive and well. May I keep the photograph?'

'Of course, I brought it for you.'

He wrapped it in a piece of newspaper and buttoned it into the pocket of his prison jacket. I glanced at my watch and began talking quickly, because time was flying. But when the two hours were up, nobody came. It wasn't until the morning that a sergeant took him away. I watched my husband leave the room, bent and skinny, shuffling like an old man and crying like a child. Colonel Andrei Sidrov, Hero of the Soviet Union, thirty-six years old.

*

The flight back to Moscow left at lunchtime. Reaction had set in by then and I cried all the way. I didn't want to see anyone, least of all Misha, so I took a room in an hotel and telephoned Abakumov. The Minister was away sick. But Varenzo had not been idle; he had arranged for Andrei to be transferred to the Petrovka prison in Kazan, and put in a plea for clemency.

'It might help if you applied as well,' he told me, so I prepared a plea before I left Moscow and addressed it to Chairman Shvernik personally.

Andrei's transfer came through on 4 November. I took the day off and went shopping for all the luxuries I could lay hands on. The prison was in an old Tartar castle. The policeman on the gate wasn't at all impressed by my uniform or my KGB card.

'You may see your husband for a quarter of an hour, but not today. Tomorrow at the earliest. And what have you got in that suitcase?'

When I opened it his eyes grew wide, and he reached for his rule book.

'Roast chicken – not allowed. Cigarettes – not allowed. Wine – not allowed. Oranges – certainly not allowed. Where did you get them, anyway?'

'I suppose talking during visiting time is not allowed either!' I snapped furiously. I went straight to my boss at the KGB office.

'Comrade Major, I have to interrogate some foreign prisoners at the Petrovka. May I have a pass for the commandant?'

In this way I was able to come and go freely and use the interrogation room at any time. Nobody bothered about the suitcase. I took Alik once, but he was terrified of the strange thin man whom he was supposed to call 'Papasha', and it wasn't a success.

Eventually, of course, the commandant sent for me.

'You had special permission to come here and talk to foreign prisoners. But I'm told that you always send for the same man, who is in fact a Soviet citizen.'

I didn't try to hide anything, but I pulled rank for all I was worth, slapping down on the commandant's desk the letters I had in my bag from Artillery Marshal Varenzo. They were wonderfully effective.

'This is a different matter altogether, Comrade Pushkova. I had no idea your husband had such influential connections. If I can be of any assistance, you have only to mention it.'

From then on, I took hot meals for Andrei to the prison every day, and he gradually began to gain strength. But nothing was heard about any pardon.

One night I was woken by the telephone ringing. It was the prison commandant; Andrei was very ill and I should go over straight away.

'What's the matter?'

'I don't know; it's his stomach. He's had a haemorrhage and he's in great pain.'

I got a surgeon from the Zelenodolsk hospital to go with me. In the prison sick bay, Andrei was on a stretcher covered with a sheet as if he was already dead. The commandant had got hold of the chief surgeon of Kazan hospital, and the two consultants spoke to each other in low, urgent voices for a few minutes. Then one of them came to me.

'Your husband is suffering from a perforated ulcer, comrade. We ought to operate at once, but he won't come through it unless he has a blood transfusion first. We shall have to find a donor.'

'That's all right; I have the same blood group. Let's get started!'

A few minutes later, Andrei and I were lying side by side in the operating theatre and blood was flowing from my body into his.

*

I stayed in the prison sick bay for a week, until Andrei was off the danger list. Then it was time for my routine visit to Moscow, another opportunity to press the case for Andrei's release. But Varenzo said that everything possible had been done, and could only advise patience; and Abakumov was in a sanatorium on the Black Sea. I decided to approach Shvernik direct. After all, he had helped me before. As soon as I had an hour to spare I made my way to the yellow Executive Committee building.

One glance at the queues of petitioners and I knew I should never get near the Chairman in the three days I could stay in Moscow. I asked an attendant if there was a quicker way.

'Why, no. You must wait your turn like everyone else. But don't imagine that you'll see Chairman Shvernik personally. How could he possibly give time to all these people! You'll be allowed to state your case to the official on duty – when you reach the head of the queue.'

I was dismayed, but not beaten. Next day I went to Central Office and issued myself with a red armband labelled 'Duty Officer' and wrote myself out a pass to the building. This time I avoided the waiting rooms and found my way, with a few carefully-worded enquiries, to the wide staircase, the red-carpeted corridor, and the ante-room to Shvernik's office.

The man at the large desk where Misha had once sat told me I couldn't possibly see the Chairman personally. I showed him my red card, and the letters from Varenzo and Abakumov. I also gave him my nicest smile. Reluctantly, he picked up the telephone.

The great office was just as I remembered it, and my knees were trembling as they had before. Shvernik looked up briefly from the papers on his desk.

'What is your problem, my dear?'

'Comrade Chairman, you helped me once; you saved my son's life.'

He gave me his full attention, but it was obvious that he didn't remember me.

'I wrote to you from the Butirka prison, and I was brought here and I made you a confession. Minister Abakumov was with you.'

At last his eyes lit up. 'Ah yes, I remember now! The little German girl. You have certainly changed to your advantage, my dear. And what can I do for you this time?'

'I am asking you now to save the life of my husband. He is still in prison; he is ill; he has never committed any crime!'

The expression of fatherly interest on Shvernik's face was replaced by one of sorrow. Either he felt a genuine concern for each of the millions whose lives he controlled – or he was a very good actor. I held my breath.

'Bring me the Sidrov file,' he said to his secretary. He went through it with some care, asking questions and making notes. Then he stood up and shook me by the hand.

'You shall have your husband back, comrade.'

As I left the office, blinded with tears, I heard him say to the secretary: 'Take a letter.'

CHAPTER EIGHTEEN

Tears for a Tyrant

Andrei was released on 30 December, 1951. Twenty-four hours later, his parents arrived from Gorki and New Year's Eve was celebrated as never before. Then we had a month's holiday on the Black Sea, at government expense, from which Andrei returned looking tanned and fit and with his hair a reasonable length again. He was reinstated in the army with full honours, given a flat in Kazan and a job at the missile base under construction nearby, and 66,000 roubles compensation. Suddenly, the state couldn't do enough for us! But Andrei's parents suffered a disaster; their house in Gorki was burnt to the ground. It seemed an ideal solution for them to move into my house in Zelenodolsk and take charge of little Alik.

We decided to spend the compensation money on building a dacha on the banks of the Volga where we could spend summer week-ends. Life was full and marvellous again, and it no longer made any sense for me to be working full-time and studying in the evenings. I put in an application to be released from the KGB, explaining that my first duty was to look after my husband and son.

As a result, I was summoned to Moscow by telephone. Abakumov received me himself, no longer the infatuated elderly cavalier but a very angry man.

'Comrade Pushkova,' he thundered, 'do you think the KGB is a charitable institution? Did you imagine you could leave us as soon as we had rehabilitated your husband? Have you still not understood that the honour of working for the State Security Service has been conferred on you for life, with no alternative but disgrace?'

The scar glowed crimson on his pale cheek. He handed me a prepared statement. In it I undertook to complete my studies in Kazan and to carry out all orders issued by Central Office without raising any objections. There was nothing I could do but sign. It was the Minister's last official act. Next day he returned to the sanatorium, a dying man.

Misha was waiting for me outside the office. As usual, he knew everything.

'Didn't I tell you, Lenotchka, right at the beginning, there's no such thing as resignation!'

He told me he was being posted to Germany. He asked if I was happy. I assured him that I was, and wished him luck. But he wouldn't let go of my hand.

'One of these days, my love, we'll be together in Berlin. And that's a promise!'

'Not a hope, comrade!'

*

The dacha was finished at midsummer and we gave a house-warming party. Andrei invited all his family, and they all came. I had never got on well with his brothers, who were rabid communists and had regarded me as frivolous and extravagant when we were first married. Now, I couldn't forget that they had kept well away from both of us until Andrei was back in official favour.

I invited Misha's mother, who had often written saying how much she would love to see Alik again. But when we met her at the station, Misha was there as well, carrying a great basket of red roses.

'I didn't think Mamushka ought to travel by herself,' he explained.

That night Andrei asked me, 'Did you have an affair with this Tshernikov fellow?'

'Whatever makes you think that?'

'He behaves as if he owns you.'

'I have to be grateful to him. When we got out of prison, he did everything possible for Alik and me.'

How could I tell Andrei the truth? Ever since his release, I had noticed, he had been inordinately jealous and suspicious of everything I did.

Next evening, during the party, there was a deplorable incident. I had gone out on to the balcony to enjoy the cool breeze from the river, when Misha came up to me and started an urgent whispering.

'You're not as happy as you make out, Lenotchka. You don't belong here and you don't fit in with that family. You've done your duty by Andrei – more than your duty – but he's not the right man for you. Come back to Moscow with me!'

He was going to kiss me, but Andrei's brother Nikolai rushed up and pushed him away.

'Don't you dare touch that woman!'

As Misha turned round, Nikolai punched him on the nose. They were both fairly drunk, I think, but Misha was by far the stronger. He picked Nikolai up and threw him over the veranda railing. Nikolai screamed, and Andrei came rushing out, revolver in hand. I flung myself in front of him. Misha had also drawn a pistol, and his mother was trying to get hold of it. Our guests were milling about, shocked and frightened; by the time order was restored the party was completely ruined.

'I won't have him in the house again,' Andrei said.

'Fine. I don't want him either. But neither do I want your brothers.'

'All right.' It was a truce, of a sort.

*

One day in late August I was on duty in the penitentiary. It was stiflingly hot, and there was nothing to do; the whole town was watching a football match. I asked my boss, Captain Olga Tshubakova, if I might take time off for a swim. The Tshubakova was hated and feared by everyone for her strictness, but I had several times brought her back lengths of dress material from Moscow, and she was quite pleasant to me in consequence. She let me go.

I collected my bathing things and hurried down to the river. There wasn't a soul about. But after I was in the water I saw two prisoners – notorious criminals known in the camp by their nicknames of 'One-eye' and 'Commissioner' – doing something with a long cord over by the stores block. I didn't think much of it; but a few minutes later, while I was lying on the bank letting the sun dry me, there was a series of explosions. The stores block was going up in flames. It contained quantities of diesel oil, paint and roofing felt, and the fire brigade never had a hope of saving it.

Afterwards, a length of fuse was found, proving that the fire had been deliberately started, and the whole prison was put on starvation rations until the culprits owned up.

I knew perfectly well who they were, of course, but I was too frightened to say anything. Andrei couldn't understand why I took the disaster so much to heart. After a few days I sent for the two men, told them what I'd seen, and tried to persuade them to confess, but all they did was threaten me with terrible consequences if I squealed on them. So I kept my mouth shut, like the coward I was, and eventually full rations had to be restored as the prisoners were getting too weak to work. No one was ever punished for the fire, but the episode later saved my life.

*

On 6 March, 1953, Andrei was on an official visit to Sverdlovsk, and I was staying with his parents in Zelenodolsk. I got up early to catch the seven o'clock train to Kazan. In the kitchen the samovar was humming and the radio was playing a solemn tune. My mother-in-law and one of Andrei's brothers were sitting at the kitchen table sobbing as if their hearts were broken.

'Oh my God, what's happened? Is it Andrei?'

They shook their heads dumbly. Exasperated, I was about to turn the radio off when the music faded and there was an announcement. Stalin was dead. The voice on the air sounded heartbroken too; the music surged into a Chopin funeral march; the kitchen was filled with the sound of weeping. Heaven knows, I had nothing to thank Stalin for, but I always succumbed to emotion easily and soon I was sobbing with the others.

Outside the townspeople were crying too. All the shops were shut, but aimless queues were still forming in front of them. Public address systems relayed solemn music, frequently interrupted by tributes to the dead leader, everywhere one went, even inside the railway carriages.

When I reached the office, the director, Major Khassim, jumped to his feet.

'Whatever's the matter, Comrade? Is there some trouble in your family?'

I blew my nose and wiped my streaming eyes.

'But don't you know, Comrade Major? Stalin is dead!'

He looked at me in utter astonishment.

'Yes, of course I know. But officers in the State Security Service can't afford to give way to emotion. Stalin was mortal, like everyone else. An able successor will be found; life will continue as before.'

There was certainly no interruption in the flow of directives from Moscow. A representative from Kazan had to go to the funeral and they chose me. Misha met me at the station, and he, too, asked what was the matter when he saw my swollen face. He roared with laughter when I told him.

'Lenotchka, you really are absurd! What a pity the old man can't see you weeping for him. He'd love the joke!'

'But everybody's crying, Misha, although they've all suffered.'

'I know they are. They wept for the tsars too, poor fools. But you're supposed to know better.'

Misha was in high spirits. He had just been promoted to full colonel and was awaiting his transfer to Berlin. He had left Sudoplatov's division and joined the counter-espionage team under General Nikolisko. Altogether, he was very pleased with himself.

'As soon as I get to Germany,' he said, 'I'll go and see your mother and tell her how well you are. You won't mind that, will you?'

I felt a terrible pang of homesickness.

*

After the pomp and ceremony of the State funeral, there was a party at Central Office. It was a gloomy affair. Sudoplatov was worried about losing his job under the new régime, and he just stood silently drinking enormous quantities of

vodka. Misha took me over to the counter-espionage division
to meet his new boss.

Colonel Shalatov was there, the officer whose face I had
slapped. When he saw me he laughed, and assured me that all
was forgiven. To Nikolisko, he said:

'You ought to recruit this girl into your department, Comrade General. She'd be just right for Berlin.'

There was no mourning for Stalin here. Vodka was flowing
freely, and everybody seemed to approve of Malenkov as the
new First Party Secretary.

'He's fat and round,' someone said. 'Such men are never
so dangerous.'

*

After the weeping, there was a period of unrest in the country.
Prisoners were being freed as a political gesture, and I met
some of them in the train going home. They seemed to think
that everything would suddenly change for the better. Andrei,
back from Sverdlovsk, was worried. The prisoners there had
staged a riot and killed the entire staff. He advised me to stay
at home.

But no sooner had Andrei left for the office than the camp
commandant rang me. Would I please come over at once and
talk to the foreign prisoners. Yes, there was a bit of trouble,
but it was under control.

Whatever control there may have been had vanished by the
time I got there. A few frightened warders were huddled by
the gate, while yelling prisoners rushed unchecked from one
hut to another. The commandant seemed appalled that I had
come. I found him in his office, with his aide and Captain
Tshubakova, desperately trying to make a phone call.

'Oh God, you're here too! If only I could get a line!'

Then he threw the receiver back into its cradle. 'Shit!' he
cursed, and that was the last word he ever uttered.

The door burst open and a horde of prisoners swept into
the office. The commandant was hit on the head; his aide was
thrown out of the window; and the fat Tshubakova was quickly
stripped naked. She was held on the floor, screaming like a
rabbit, while one after another the men raped her. I was picked
up and flung on the commandant's desk, and eager hands were

tearing at my blouse when suddenly a voice shouted above the uproar:

'Not that one, you fools!'

It was the convict 'One-eye' who had started the stores block fire He dragged me off the desk and half-carried me out of the building. At the door I glanced back at Captain Tshubakova. She was quiet now, and appeared to be unconscious. Someone was trying to ram an empty vodka bottle into her. As soon as we got outside, I was sick. 'One-eye' covered my uniform with his prison jacket and hurried me to the station. A train was waiting, and he pushed me into it.

'Get away, girl, and don't ever come back! I won't be able to save you again.'

I was in hospital for some weeks after this, with concussion, shock and a sort of nervous breakdown. Andrei had a row with Major Khassim at the KGB office and I was taken off prison work. Meanwhile, all over Russia, the Red Army had moved in to stop the rioting, and the calls for freedom were silenced with machine-gun fire.

Then the purges at the top began. Beria was arrested, charged with responsibility for all the terror of the last years of Stalin's rule, and later shot. Everyone in the KGB was worried; Misha got me transferred to the counter-espionage unit.

'At least,' he said, 'we are now among those who arrest, not those who are arrested. Seventh Division has nothing to fear.'

But the next time I saw him he looked dreadful.

'Sudoplatov was arrested yesterday!' he blurted out as we were driving from the station to his flat.

'Surely that was only to be expected?'

'Yes, I know. But I was there. They sent me on ahead so that he wouldn't suspect anything – I had no idea myself, you understand – and while we were chatting about old times, Nikolisko and Ovtshynikov rushed in and clapped handcuffs on him. And as they were marching him off, he turned to me – I'll never forget it – and said: "Misha, old friend, cover my face, please. There's no need for everybody to see." So I pulled the red cloth off the table and threw it over him. I don't know where he is now.'

Misha, the tough, experienced KGB colonel, broke down in tears. 'Oh God, I wish they'd let me go back to Germany and have nothing to do with all this!' Then he brightened up. 'That reminds me, I have a confession to make.'

He told me that he and General Nikolisko had been organizing my future. When I had taken my finals in Kazan, I was to do another course at the Dzerzhinski Academy that would qualify me for work in Germany. I could expect to be posted there in about a year from now.

'I won't go without Alik!'

'You'll be allowed to take him, don't worry.'

'And what about Andrei?'

'He'll have to make his own arrangements.'

We talked about it when I got home and Andrei gradually became quite keen on the idea. He said he would ask Varenzo for a transfer. But it was all a long way off yet; I still had exams to pass.

In November, I had a letter from Misha. He had been promoted again, to Brigadier-General. He told me that Abakumov, ill as he was, had been arrested, and so had Bowermann, and that the 'reorganization' now seemed to be over. He was just leaving for Potsdam, and he sent Andrei his regards.

CHAPTER NINETEEN

A Strange Homecoming

In May, 1954, I passed my finals at the Kazan Institute, and in June I began work at the Academy. It was an interesting course, all about espionage and counter-espionage; how to establish dead letter boxes; how to contact another agent.

'The first principle is to be inconspicuous,' the lecturer impressed on us, 'and to this end, you must always adopt the customs of the country you happen to be in. If you're working in the United States, for example, you must change your shirt every day, however extravagant that seems. In Germany, never keep your money loose in your pockets, but in a purse. Never, never give the impression that you are a military man. An officer of the Intelligence Service must look completely guileless, bourgeois, perhaps even a little naïve.' He looked round the lecture hall, saw me, and came over. 'Here, comrades, is a perfect example of what I mean.'

We were taught how to cope with lie detectors.

'Keep your eyes fixed on one particular point, a picture on the wall, or a gap in the floorboards. Answer questions only with "yes" or "no", don't move your eyes, and you'll find your pulse will keep going at a steady rate.'

It was all quite fascinating, and the reward for learning it would be the posting to Berlin. I really enjoyed that summer in Moscow. Andrei would bring Alik up sometimes for a long week-end, and he spent his annual leave in the city with me. It was an opportunity to see Varenzo about his transfer, but the Marshal was not encouraging; there were no missile bases in Germany.

When the course ended in October, I was promoted to captain and given a month's leave. Andrei had applied to join the field artillery missile division, which did have posts in Germany, but nothing had yet come through and he had to stay at his job in Kazan. Tears ran down his face as he saw Alik and me off at the station.

'Cheer up, Androusha,' I tried to console him. 'My posting's only for six months; I'll be back in May.'

He shook his head and refused to be comforted. Perhaps he knew that I was never coming back.

On 12 November, 1954, the long-distance express from Moscow crossed the border at Frankfurt-on-Oder. Almost nine years ago, I had passed this way in the opposite direction, bald-headed and crammed in a filthy cattletruck. From my luxury Pullman car I gazed out at the landscape; it hadn't changed as much as I.

We reached Berlin in the afternoon and were met by a small reception committee – Misha, my mother and Herr Cramm. Mother looked shrunken and fragile; and Herr Cramm, who had helped the family so much in the early days of war and exile, had grown old and grey and very thin. But his eyes, I noticed, were still merry and shrewd. We sat in the station buffet drinking champagne, while Mother, with Alik on her knee, gazed at me as if she couldn't believe her eyes.

'You can go to Güsten first,' Misha said, 'and settle Alik in with his grandmother. Report for duty at my office in Potsdam in a fortnight's time.'

'*Jawohl*, Comrade General!'

When our train stopped at Güsten, the platform was crowded with people and a band was playing a Russian marching song.

'What on earth's going on here?' I asked.

Herr Cramm smiled. 'I'm afraid, my dear, you'll find they're doing it for you.'

And so it was. A solemn man with a badge in his lapel presented me with a bunch of chrysanthemums and made a little speech.

'Permit me to welcome you, dear Comrade Pushkova-Wannenmacher, on behalf of the Socialist Unitarian Party of

Germany. We are all proud that a citizen of our town has become such a distinguished comrade and that she returns to us wearing the uniform of the heroic Soviet Army.'

While he was speaking, I was trying to remember where I had seen him before. I knew his voice, and that face with the long pointed nose. Suddenly it all came back to me. He was the local secretary of the German communist party who had denounced me to Jatshuk for warning his purge victims, all those years ago. Herr Bolle, his name was. Did he really think that he would get away with such a change of tune? I looked very hard into his eyes to show him that I had not forgotten.

At last we were able to relax in Mother's flat. My brother Jossi came in; he was married now with three children and he worked as an engine driver. There was so much to talk about! Father had been arrested quite soon after I'd gone and died in prison a year later. Mother had had to put up with constant questioning and harassment from Herr Bolle; Herr Cramm had lost all his property and now worked as a clerk.

I looked round the cheerful room. 'But your flat is very nice, Mamushka!'

'Yes, it is, isn't it. A year ago I was living in a tiny room in the attic. But then your friend General Tshernikov started coming to see me, in his uniform and his big official car – and after that had happened a few times Herr Bolle had me moved down here, at government expense. I didn't have to do anything except choose the furniture. It's disgusting, really.'

'The bastard!'

'Don't say that, dear. He is the regional secretary, after all, and he has very good connections among the Russians.'

'My connections are better than his, believe me!'

*

The extraordinary thing about Comrade Bolle was that he really didn't seem to remember the part he'd played in my downfall. He made no effort to keep out of my way; on the contrary, he could hardly leave me alone. Next morning he came round to invite me to a welcoming party at the town hall. The theme was to be 'German-Soviet Friendship'. Uniforms would be worn.

It turned out to be less a party than a political meeting.

The hall was packed; the press was there in force; and when I arrived I was led on to the platform where the Mayor and other dignitaries were sitting. Herr Bolle came bustling over to me.

'You are our principal speaker tonight, Comrade Pushkova. Your subject is "Life in the most liberated country in the world".'

'Don't be silly! I haven't prepared anything. Nobody warned me I should have to speak.'

'That doesn't matter in the least, Comrade. We've written the speech for you.'

While the Mayor was having his say, I glanced through the typescript Bolle had given me. It was nothing but a fulsome eulogy to the Soviet Union, worse even than some I had had to listen to in the course of my work. I couldn't bring myself to speak a word of it. The Mayor introduced me and I got to my feet, still wondering what on earth to do.

'Just read it, will you!' Bolle hissed behind me. I turned round very deliberately and handed the speech back to him. Then I faced my audience and told them about the individual Russian people I had known, in prison, at university, in the capital and in the provinces. I spoke of their friendliness and their hunger for knowledge, their love of music and literature, their warmth and generosity. I made no mention of the system, Party policy, or anything political at all. At the end there was thunderous applause.

Comrade Bolle didn't even have enough pride to be angry. Next morning he came to show me the press reports; my picture was in all the papers. He told me that my speech had been broadcast on the radio, and that the Party secretaries of Halle, Leipzig and Meinigen had already enquired if I would be willing to go and speak at their meetings.

'Sorry – not interested.'

*

The following Sunday, while Mother was getting ready for church, I suddenly decided to go with her.

'But surely you can't, being a Soviet officer!'

'Rubbish! Alik can come, too.'

We dressed him up in his best clothes, and after the service we visited Father's grave.

Two hours later the doorbell rang. Bolle was there with two officials from district Party headquarters. They insisted on coming into the flat.

'Comrade Pushkova,' Bolle began pompously, 'it has been brought to our attention that you went to church this morning.'

'Correct. Your spies are very efficient.'

'I could hardly believe it! Don't you know that no Party member is allowed to enter a church?'

'That may be the case for German communists. In Russia we have no such rule.'

'Surely that can't be true!' Bolle tried to start a discussion on the antagonism between communism and the Church, but I had already got the door open and it was all I could do not to kick them as they filed out.

Another time, I had gone to Berlin with Herr Cramm, and the train that was to take us back to Güsten was absolutely filthy; the carriages were ancient, with torn upholstery and broken windows. I complained to the guard. He looked me over contemptuously.

'Not good enough for you, Comrade? We're all the same now, you know. Go on – get in!'

I wasn't in uniform, but I did have my KGB card with me, and I waved it under his nose.

'According to regulations, every train has to have at least one first class carriage for members of the Soviet administration. Where is it, please?'

The guard's tone changed from arrogance to servility in a flash. When he had finished apologizing, he rushed to the station master's office, and the train was kept waiting for half an hour while a first class saloon car was found and shunted on to it. The guard escorted us to it and saluted as we climbed aboard. As the train was leaving, he had an afterthought.

'May I just see the gentleman's papers, please?'

'No, you may not!' I told him firmly and slammed the window shut.

Herr Cramm had hugely enjoyed the whole incident.

'Oh Helga, little girl,' he chuckled, 'you certainly have come on!'

Part Three

CHAPTER TWENTY

The Pleasures of Revenge

But it was with a heavy heart that I travelled to Potsdam to begin my new job. The excitement of coming home had worn off and I was thoroughly disillusioned by what I'd seen of communist Germany. These were not the heroic people that the Hitler Youth organizations were supposed to have turned out; apathy and corruption alternated with slavish obedience to Russia.

Misha was bubbling with energy and enthusiasm and my depression had lifted by the time he took me out to dinner after a day of conferences. It was good to be working together again; I was really very fond of him.

Over dinner he briefed me on my first assignment. A Soviet military unit stationed at Burg was suffering from a mysterious, and usually fatal, outbreak of suspected food poisoning. The barracks kitchens were staffed by Germans; I was to find out whether any of them were Western agents who might be responsible for the poisoning.

Burg was quite near Güsten. I visited the military hospital and carefully observed the symptoms of the sick men. Then I went to Güsten to see a doctor there whom I knew and trusted. As I described the symptoms, he shook his head and smiled.

'These Russians! They're delightful people, but they see sabotage in everything. Don't they know that there's a lot of rabies in the woods around here? Listen – one of the effects of the disease is a panic fear of water. Show a glass of water to one of those poor fellows and see if I'm right.'

When the next 'poisoned' patient was admitted to the ward, I did just that, and he screamed so loud that all the nurses came running. Laboratory tests confirmed the diagnosis.

Misha was very pleased with me. 'I always knew you were an efficient girl, Lenotchka. You only need to be given the right assignments.'

'Just as long as I'm not required to kill anybody, you mean!'

'You won't be next time, either, but it may not be quite as simple.' He took a thick file from the safe. 'This concerns the Soviet headquarters in Hettstedt. The officers there are sending home crates of valuables – furs, silver, jewellery, china and pictures. The economics officer, Major Shovin, took a whole railway carriage full when he went on leave.'

'Well, why don't you just arrest the lot of them?'

'We can't very well arrest the entire staff, can we? And we haven't any evidence. We want to know how it's done. You are to go there as economics officer in place of Major Shovin. Make as many contacts as possible, both Russian and German, and give the impression that you are a very lively comrade ready for any lark, particularly if there's something in it for you. Keep your eyes and ears open and report to me regularly.'

Hettstedt was a pretty little town in the foothills of the Harz mountains; the Soviet and German authorities were on excellent terms and enjoyed a swinging social life. The Russian commandant, Colonel Rapuchin, lived in considerable splendour in half of a villa belonging to the East German President, Wilhelm Pieck, and I was allowed to occupy the other half on condition I moved out for the President's rare visits. I sent for Mother and Alik; she had to pose as my housekeeper, of course, but it was almost a holiday for her.

Another couple prominent for their hospitality were Lotte and Hans Vogt. He was chief of the German security service, SSD, and their house, too, was full of treasures. Both Frau Lotte and Rapuchin's wife dressed expensively and seemed to own a lot of jewellery. I became as friendly as possible with them, but, apart from a little fiddling over the soldiers' rations, I couldn't find any irregularities in the administration.

It was noticeable though, that on the one occasion that Wilhelm Pieck did visit the town, the life-style of its leading citizens suddenly changed. The President was known to be a man of simple tastes, and for as long as he was there the Rapuchin and Vogt households had simple tastes too. Neither of the wives wore any furs or jewellery.

In the end Frau Lotte gave the game away. I was having dinner with them and she was talking about a visit she had paid that afternoon to a local doctor's house, for a private consultation. It was impossible to change the subject; she went on all evening about what beautiful antiques he had, what fine pictures and carpets.

'Utter luxury wherever one looked. Did you know, Hans, that his wife has a real mink?'

'No.'

Frau Lotte seemed overexcited. I noticed she she was drinking rather a lot. Presently she went and sat on her husband's knee.

'Listen, Hans, wasn't Dr Keller a Nazi?'

'No, darling, I would have known if he had been.'

'Isn't there anything else you could pin on him?'

Comrade Vogt glanced uneasily at me. 'I really don't know what you mean, my love.'

'Oh come on, you needn't worry about Jelena, she's our friend. Aren't you, dear? And wouldn't you like something nice for yourself?'

There was no need even to tell a lie. 'Oh yes,' I answered eagerly, 'I've been dying for a chance like this!'

Vogt chuckled. 'In that case, we shall have to fix Keller, if only for Jelena's sake.'

He and his wife discussed the problem quite cold-bloodedly. They decided to wait until a woman was taken to hospital with a miscarriage, and then to suggest that it might be an illegal abortion.

'The commandant will accuse him of the same thing – separately of course. He'll go then, you'll see.'

'But if he just runs away, how can he be made to pay up?'

'He doesn't have to. He's left everything behind, hasn't he?'

Less than a week later, Rapuchin telephoned me late one night and told me to come out on a house search. The owner, Dr Keller, had made an illegal flight from the Republic.

'But house searches aren't part of my duties.'

'I promise you you'll find it worth while. I'll pick you up in ten minutes.'

That gave me just time to telephone Misha. At the house,

the Vogts were already packing things into suitcases. But Frau
Lotte was distraught.

'I can't find the mink coat anywhere! She must have taken
it with her.'

Good for her, I thought.

We were all still there when the ZIM limousine brought
Misha and three other KGB officers, and my job was over.

*

Mother was completely mystified.

'What on earth was it that brought the general here in the
middle of the night?'

I gave her the gist of it, but she wasn't impressed.

'That's nothing new. Herr Bolle has been doing the same
thing in Güsten for years.'

'Mother! However do you know that?'

'His wife told me.'

'How could she? What an awful thing to do!'

'Oh well, he's unfaithful to her, you know, and she's very
unhappy.'

'Who's his mistress?'

'Look, I don't know anything about politics and I don't want
to get involved. You'd better ask her yourself.'

Frau Bolle was only too ready to talk and I soon had all the
information I needed. I checked her statements and prepared
the dossier, and then I handed it to Misha.

'This is the man who got me sent to Siberia.'

'Right! How long were you in prison first?'

I told him.

'I'll see that he does exactly the same. And what was your
sentence?'

'Ten years.' I still shuddered at the memory. Misha rubbed
his hands.

'Fine. Herr Bolle will get at least as much for this little lot.'

*

At the end of May, 1955, our offices were moved to 'Little
Moscow', otherwise Karlshorst, a restricted area in the suburbs
where all Soviet personnel working in Berlin were to be housed.
It had a ten-foot wire fence around it, and patrolling guards,

but those were its only resemblances to a prison camp. Inside, we enjoyed every sort of Western luxury – shops and restaurants, hairdressers, tennis courts, cinemas, an open-air swimming pool and a theatre. I had a delightful house and garden to myself, and Mother and Alik were with me. An elderly German pensioner tended the garden; a Russian maid called Zenya looked after the house. Life was really very pleasant, apart from the miserable letters I kept getting from Andrei. It was true, I'd promised him I'd be back in May; but when I reminded Misha that my six months were up, he only laughed.

'Do you really think we'd send you back when you're doing so well, and when you've just found your way around? Anyway, be honest, would you willingly exchange Karlshorst for Kazan?

The answer to that question did nothing to appease my conscience. But even in our secluded garden suburb, things were not always what they seemed.

My gardener and I had established a little ritual. Every day before I went to the office he would come to the front door and present me with a posy, always with the words:

'Good morning, lady, I've cut you some flowers.'

In return, I'd given him a pack of Western cigarettes or a few coffee beans. One day I was called to Misha's office. He was standing by his desk with a bunch of tulips in his hand.

'Good morning, lady, I've cut you some flowers.'

His broad grin told me it was a joke of some kind, but for a few seconds I was completely baffled.

'What are you talking about?'

'Well, if this old geezer brings you flowers every morning, I don't see why I shouldn't do it sometimes.'

'Yes, but how did you know? Am I being watched?'

'Not officially. But the last tenant of that house was, and we forgot to disconnect the bugging device before you moved in. So every time anyone steps on the doormat, the tape recorder starts running. The officer in charge of surveillance sent me the tape yesterday.'

I burst into hysterical weeping. Ever since I'd found that microphone in the Moscow flat, I'd been allergic to bugging devices.

155

'Oh Misha, how could you joke about it? Don't you remember how frightened we were?'

'Of course, but that was in Stalin's day, and I was only a major.'

'And now Stalin's dead and you're a general, but the bugging still goes on!'

'I keep telling you – it was a mistake.'

It was a long time before I allowed myself to be mollified.

Another day I discovered that my wardrobe had been searched. Zenya, the friendly Russian maid, was the only possible suspect and I taxed her with it. She denied it at first, but in the end admitted she had had a look, out of curiosity.

'And what did you take?'

'Nothing, Comrade Captain!'

'Are you sure? I shall have to report this, anyway.'

As I was lifting the telephone, Zenya put her hand over mine and pressed the receiver back in its cradle. Her whole manner and appearance had subtly altered; she didn't seem like a maid any more.

'Just a moment, Comrade. Perhaps I had better tell you the truth.'

'I think that's a very good idea.'

Zenya ran up to her bedroom and came back with a red KGB card. Inside was a photograph of her in uniform, and the name, Lieutenant Zenya Markiyeva, 5th Division.

I handed it back to her with a stiff smile.

'And who gave you the order to snoop around my house?'

'I'm afraid I can't tell you any more, Captain.'

Misha's smile was rather strained, too, when I told him about it. 'Fifth Division, that's civilian intelligence, General Ovtshynikov. Of course! He recommended the girl to me!'

'For heaven's sake, Misha, I've had enough of this, I'm leaving!'

'Don't be silly. How can you? Anyway, it's not so terrible. You'll have to do without a maid, but your mother's there; you'll manage all right.'

He put an arm round my shoulders. 'And now I'd like to talk to you about your next assignment. It's a very important one. Somehow we've got to get more of the Americans in West Germany working for us.'

CHAPTER TWENTY-ONE

The Youngest Recruit

I was attached to the trade mission at the Soviet Embassy in Unter den Linden. I wore the shoulder straps of an Engineer Corps officer; but my real job was to attract any Americans that came my way, and, if the chance arose, to allow myself to be recruited as a Western agent.

The first opportunity came during the state visit of Krushchev and Bulganin in July. After the speeches and ceremonies there was a reception at the embassy, attended by senior officers of the occupying forces of each zone of the city.

Misha had briefed me carefully. It was a more dangerous game he was asking me to play than anything I'd done before. Too friendly a manner would arouse suspicion; I must be aloof, yet susceptible.

'It's up to you, Lenotchka. One thing you can be quite sure of – they'll approach you of their own accord. You won't have to lift a finger!'

He was quite right. An American Lieutenant-Colonel came up to me at the buffet and started heaping goodies on to my plate. Within five minutes he was offering to show me the sights of West Berlin. It was all much too quick for me; I lost my nerve and fled to the ladies' room.

Misha had observed the whole encounter, but he wasn't quite as angry as I had feared.

'It does take a bit of getting used to, I know. They've no finesse. Never mind. You know what to expect now. Go to the Leipzig Trade Fair.'

At the fair, I was so fascinated by the stands in the exhibition halls that I almost forgot why I was there. A Russian woman beside me was gazing at the fur coats on display.

'Oh God,' she murmured, 'if only I could afford an ocelot coat like that one!'

I had been thinking much the same thing; we got talking and strolled on together. We stopped again at a display of Swiss watches, and while we were admiring them a man's voice spoke behind us.

'Excuse me, ladies, I couldn't help overhearing your conversation. Perhaps I could be of service?'

I turned round and looked at him carefully. He was expensively dressed in Western style, yet his Russian was perfect. He must be a successful emigré. These, we had been taught at the Academy, were of particular interest to the KGB. The woman I had been talking to evidently thought it was just a pick-up; she vanished into the crowd.

'Have I insulted your friend? I didn't mean to. I really can get you a Swiss watch, if you like.'

'I'd love one, but I can only pay in East German marks.'

'Don't worry about payment! I'd be only too pleased to do a favour to someone from the old country.'

Now we were getting somewhere! Not everybody offered free Swiss watches to a perfect stranger.

'Think about it,' he went on. 'Here's my telephone number; I'll be there till the end of the fair. Just ask for Yourka.'

I phoned Misha and asked what I should do.

'Ring him, of course. Agree to any proposal he makes. You're a teacher at the Russian school in Karlshorst; you're not very well off; you're mad about Western luxury goods and you do see a few faults in the Soviet system. Okay? Keep in touch.'

Yourka presented me with a beautiful watch and waved away the East German marks I offered him.

'Perhaps you will return the favour some time.'

'I could get you some Russian books,' I offered eagerly.

'Well, yes, fine. I'm sure we'll come to some arrangement. Incidentally, I have a friend in Berlin who deals in furs. What would you say to an ocelot coat like that one you were admiring the other day?'

'Oh, but that would be . . . '

'I've told you, you would only have to do me a small favour occasionally. Give me your Berlin telephone number.'

*

He rang a week later. He had spoken to his friend about the coat. There was a ticket for me at the box office of a certain theatre, for a certain performance. He looked forward to seeing me there.

'Good!' said Misha, 'I'll be there too. It's time I knew what he looks like.'

My seat was between a young girl and a very old man. Misha and his aide, Major Arlov, were sitting four rows behind looking bored and disappointed. As I got up to leave after the show the girl whispered:

'Yourka sends his regards; he couldn't make it tonight. He wants you to come over and be measured for the coat. I could fetch you; would next Saturday do?' We quickly arranged a time and place and then she slipped away.

'They're certainly careful,' Misha grumbled, 'but go anyway. Arlov will follow you.'

On Saturday afternoon the girl, who was called Irmgard, took me to the zoo. Yourka was looking at the lions. We chatted for a bit, and then he looked at his watch and said:

'Let's go and have tea with a friend of mine, the Countess Ostrova. She's an interesting woman; I think you'll enjoy meeting her. And I want to see her about some ocelot skins she's keeping for me.'

As we piled into a taxi I saw Arlov rushing to take the next one in the rank.

The Countess lived in Spandau. She was a small, elegant woman of about fifty, and her flat was full of treasures from the old régime. There was even a portrait of Tsar Nicholas II on the wall. We had tea from a silver samovar and talked about Russia, past and present. I ventured a little guarded criticism of the communist system and saw my hosts exchange satisfied glances. Then Yourka produced the ocelot skins and measured me for the coat, and the conversation turned to clothes and fashions. It was a very pleasant afternoon – but I came away without the faintest idea of what I was supposed to do for them.

I didn't find out until the fourth visit, when the coat was finished. Once again I offered to pay for it, in instalments, in East German marks.

'No,' said Yourka firmly, 'the coat is yours. We'd just be grateful if you would mail a few letters for us. By the diplomatic postal service, I mean, to avoid the censorship.'

'Of course I will; I know how I can arrange that. But is that really all, for such a beautiful coat?'

When Yourka looked enquiringly at the Countess I wondered if I had overdone my air of innocence. Apparently not, as he went on to say:

'Jelena Kirilovna, we know you quite well now and I think we can put our cards on the table. We are members of NWS - the National Workers' Society – which aims at freeing the Russian people from communist rule. There will be more letters to post from time to time; it's absolutely invaluable for us to be able to get uncensored material through to our agents in Moscow. Do you understand now?'

The only thing I didn't understand was how the NWS could afford to be so generous; most of these underground dissident groups were as poor as church mice. But later I met another of the Countess's visitors, Mr von Grau, a wealthy American who had no inhibitions about mentioning money. He spoke good Russian, had a German name, and was altogether an enigmatic character. However I soon found out that his American dollars were financing the society.

I reported to Misha at Karlshorst.

'Ah, the National Workers' Society!' he said, 'I know about them. They're a bunch of fascists, idealists and fools. They come into Ovtshynikov's province.'

It didn't make any difference. I had to go on working for them, crossing into West Berlin to get their letters which were opened and photocopied at Karlshorst and then sent on. The contents seemed very harmless and Ovtshynikov's experts never did succeed in breaking the code. But the addressees' names were carefully noted, and the general was satisfied that he would eventually get the lot of them.

In those days, of course, there was no Berlin Wall and it was comparatively easy to cross from one zone into another. But in my role as a schoolteacher I was supposed not to understand any German, and the girl Irmgard always came to fetch me and to speak for me at the checkpoints. I became quite friendly with her, and profoundly hated the part I was playing.

*

Misha was contemptuous of the NWS and far more interested in the CIA. I had to attend every official party where American guests might be expected.

'Almost all the fellows who squeeze our hands and slap our backs so heartily belong to the CIA,' he insisted.

'Just as any Russian who talks nicely to an American belongs to the KGB.'

'Well, yes,' Misha laughed, 'that's the way the cookie crumbles – as our friends would say.'

'It's idiotic! They're after our agents and we are after theirs. If both sides agreed to lay off, we could have a lot of time and money.'

'Never mind the feminine logic, there's a good girl. Just do as you're told!'

As usual, I had no choice. My next encounter was the result of a lucky accident. The Leningrad Symphony Orchestra came to give a concert in West Berlin. It was something of a cultural occasion; everybody was there, and I, on duty of course, was escorted by Major Arlov and Colonel Shalatov. During the interval, I tripped on the stairs and the heel of my shoe broke off. I sat on a window-sill nursing a twisted ankle while my escorts went to try and borrow some shoes for me, and before long a tall, crew-cut, expensively-dressed man came up and asked me, in Russian, if he could be of any assistance. This might be interesting; I decided to try a little flattery.

'Thank you, Comrade, but I don't really think you could do anything.'

'Comrade? I'm not Russian, you know; I'm American.'

'Would you believe it! I'd never have guessed; your Russian is perfect!'

He looked at the heel-less shoe in my hand.

'That's easily fixed. There's a heel bar not far from here. I'll send someone out with it and in ten minutes it'll be good as new.'

I had never heard of heel bars – a recent American invention

– so my amazement and gratitude were quite genuine. He went away with the shoe and was back in no time; evidently his rank was fairly high if he could command a messenger so easily in the middle of a concert.

'It shouldn't be too long now.' He helped me to my feet. 'Let's wait in the bar.'

At that moment Arlov returned. Seeing us together, he walked unhesitatingly straight on up the stairs.

The American introduced himself as Mr Mentor. In a very few minutes, he was offering to show me West Berlin.

'Oh, that would be exciting! But I'd never get permission to go out with you.'

'Why not? Because I'm from the States? We're supposed to be your allies, you know.'

'Well, you might be a spy or something.'

Mr Mentor guffawed with laughter. 'Say, young lady – do I look like a spy?'

I gazed trustingly into his eyes. 'How should I know? I've never seen one.'

He was quite doubled up with mirth. 'Anyway, if I were, what state secrets would you be able to betray to me?'

'Well, none really.' I was every inch the helpless little woman. 'But my husband is a missiles expert. I mean, that's supposed to be pretty secret, isn't it?'

The laughter was cut off as if I'd thrown a switch. Then he recovered himself and added a nervous giggle.

'I hadn't realized you were married. That sure is a pity, but congratulations on having such a distinguished husband. Missiles are way out of my class, and if you did talk about them I shouldn't understand a single word. I'm just a doctor myself.'

If you're a doctor, I thought, then I'm the President of the United States.

The bell rang for the end of the interval, and the bar quickly emptied. There was still no sign of my shoe.

'Let's stay and have another drink,' Mr Mentor said. 'You can't very well run around in stockinged feet.' He ordered highballs; I thought they tasted like medicine.

Presently a young man brought my shoe, still unmended, and a new pair which fitted me perfectly. Mr Mentor explained

162

that the heel bar was closed and asked me to accept the new pair.

'I don't know how to thank you!'

'Then let me tell you.'

All I had to do was agree to a date with him – Saturday afternoon at the zoo.

*

'Can't they ever think of anywhere else?' sighed Misha when I reported. 'At the zoo you can find agents of all the secret services in the world. Every other tree is a dead letter box. Well – have a good time, Lenotchka, you'll be tailed all the way.'

I was strolling around the zoo with Mr Mentor, perfectly relaxed, almost enjoying the game of cat and mouse we were playing with each other, when suddenly I saw Alik. He was aiming a toy gun at the monkey cage. Misha was beyond him, apparently photographing the boy but actually, as I well knew, taking pictures of me and my companion. Then Alik turned and pointed his gun at Mr Mentor.

'Don't do that,' Misha said, 'you must never shoot at people.'

Alik obediently lowered the gun. Misha grinned at me, took the boy's hand and walked away. I stared after them. Alik had given no sign of recognizing me; normally he would have rushed up shouting with delight.

'What's the matter?' Mr Mentor asked, 'you look quite pale. Are you frightened of your own compatriots?'

It was the cue I needed. 'Well, yes, I suppose I am. I shouldn't really be here, you know.'

'Oh, forget it! You always meet a lot of Russians on this side. They come over to shop in the big department stores. That guy must have bought the gun for his little boy here.'

That guy, I reflected grimly, has something coming to him when I get home!

We completed the circuit of the zoo.

'What would you like to do now? You've only to say.'

'Would there be time to see an American movie?'

'Just about!' He took me to a Mickey Mouse film at Zoo Station. Alik would have loved it.

'Next time you come across,' said Mr Mentor as we waited

for my train, 'we'll go on a shopping spree.' He took a package out of his pocket. 'This is just a little something to remind you of our afternoon together.' It was a pair of gold earrings.

'Oh, but I can't.'

'Really, I insist. It has been a great pleasure.' He thrust the package into my hands as the train came in.

At home in Karlshorst, Misha was playing with Alik.

'Mamushka,' Alik cried, 'did you see me shoot the bad man at the zoo?'

I kissed him and took him to Mother's room; then I went back to deal with Misha. He showed me the photographs.

'For our crime files!'

'Next time you do that,' I said, 'I'll introduce you. "This is my superior officer, General Tshernikov of Seventh Division, KGB. I'm sure you'd like to meet him." I promise you I'll do it!'

Misha raised his hands. 'All right, never again. But wasn't it a good idea? And didn't Alik behave like a proper little KGB man?'

'How did you do it?'

'I just told him that if the bad man thought we knew you, he'd take you away.'

It was the skill of Alik's performance that upset me as much as anything.

CHAPTER TWENTY-TWO

The Double Game

Just as Irmgard took me to and from the meetings with Yourka and the Countess, so a youth called Alfred escorted me through the checkpoint to Mr Mentor. A week later he fetched me for the shopping expedition. I was equipped with a mini camera in the lid of my compact and a tape recorder sewn into the shoulder padding of my jacket. Mr Mentor had a friend with him, whom he introduced as Mr Smith. I don't think he recognized me, but I knew him at once as the Lieutenant-Colonel from whom I had fled at the Krushchev reception. The first thing I did when we met at the Gedächtniskirche was to powder my nose.

For the rest of the afternoon I had no need to act a part. The shopping was a real treat, and when I had spent all my own money, more was thrust into my hands. Alfred trotted behind us carrying the parcels.

At the end of it all, Mr Mentor invited me home for dinner. 'My wife is so looking forward to meeting you,' he said; and I expect she was; the woman who greeted us was as much his wife as I, so often, had been Misha's. As we sat down to dinner, I activated my shoulder tape recorder and looked around for a bugging device in the room. There was nothing obvious, so I dropped my bag on the floor. Bending to pick it up, I located the microphone, taped rather untidily on the underside of the table.

I don't know what the CIA bosses thought of their tape, but Misha was very pleased with mine.

RED SPY AT NIGHT

'I think you'll get an offer soon. Keep going!'

In the end it was Mr Smith who made the offer. He gave me a huge bottle of French perfume at our next meeting and waved my protests aside.

'Maybe you could do me a little favour some time.'

He told me that his hobby was military history. Any Russian military document would be of interest, but his great ambition was to see a copy of the Strelkovoi Oustva.

'I don't suppose you even know what that is,' he added with a smile.

As it happened, I did. It was a list of all the weapons in current use by the Soviet armed forces, a top secret document.

'I only need it for half an hour and then you can take it back. It's worth three thousand dollars to you.'

*

'Three thousand dollars,' Misha mused. 'That's a very fair price. Here you are.' He opened his safe and took out a small red book. 'It's not the real one, but they'll never know.'

Mr Smith was genuinely surprised when I produced the book from my handbag.

'Well, I'll be . . . You are a clever girl!' He disappeared with it into the next room, and when he came back, he counted out thirty 100-dollar bills.

'There's plenty more where that came from. You can earn yourself a lot of dough with us, young lady!' He playfully slapped me on the back, and I had to twist sharply to avoid my tape recorder getting damaged.

After that I was constantly on the move, crossing from East to West Berlin with either Alfred or Irmgard, working simultaneously with the NWS and the CIA, always shadowed by the KGB. I brought back photographs of everyone I met, and tapes of every conversation. It was a tense, tiring life, but in a way I quite enjoyed it. I liked the sense of importance it gave me, and, at least as far as the Americans were concerned, of being always one jump ahead of them. It was like a game that I was rather good at – until Irmgard was killed.

It was in the spring of 1956. Misha's time in Germany was up and he had gone back to Moscow. He had told me he was going to apply for a transfer to the diplomatic service. 'And if I get it, Lenotchka, I shall want to have a serious talk with you about our future.' I was left wondering what he meant by that.

I was also left very much alone, as I realized when General Ovtshynikov casually said:

'I wonder who the NWS will send to meet you this time.'

'What do you mean? It's always Irmgard.'

'Not any more – she's dead.'

He might have been talking about his neighbour's dog. I kept myself rigidly under control. 'What happened?'

'A car drove up on the pavement and hit her. She died at once.'

'And how do you know about it?'

'It is our business to know these things.'

That same evening, Yourka telephoned and, using a code we had worked out for messages, told me I should have to cross into West Berlin by myself. It wasn't difficult; the guards knew me by now. But when I got to the meeting, Yourka, too, told me about the accident as if a dog had been run over. The car, apparently, had backed away and driven straight off.

'But didn't anyone get the number?'

'Oh yes, several people did. But the car wasn't registered in Berlin, or anywhere else for that matter. Well now, let's get on with the meeting, shall we?'

I never did find out which side was responsible, though that wasn't important. But I suddenly saw, very clearly, exactly what I was doing. This was no gentlemanly battle of wits, fought out in aristocratic drawing-rooms and round the dining tables of wealthy Americans. It was a squalid feud which I wasn't even meant to understand. Far from playing a leading part, I was a pawn, like Irmgard, and sooner or later I, too, would become superfluous to one lot of butchers or the other. Abakumov was no longer around to save me, nor Sudoplatov to give me one more chance, and Misha, that blatant careerist, would not mourn me for long.

After six years in espionage I still hadn't learnt to hide my feelings and General Ovtshynikov soon noticed that I was unhappy. His reaction was to order the guards not to let Alik out of the restricted area of Karlshorst. When I found that I couldn't take the boy into town with me one morning, I stormed into the general's office.

'This is absurd! Mother's not well and I can't leave Alik with her all the time.'

'I'm sorry to hear that. You mustn't be burdened with domestic problems. Send your mother home to Güsten and I'll get a nursemaid for you.'

A few days later Zenya moved back into the house. If I had thought about escaping, the general's tactics were as effective as putting me in chains.

But after this I did think about escaping, more and more. One day a colleague who was going on leave brought me a sackful of official documents.

'Could you possibly take these to the incinerator for me, Jelena Kirilovna? I'll miss my train otherwise.'

'Yes, of course. Leave the bag here. I'll deal with it.'

It was full of classified information, including the latest Strelkovoi Oustva. I took that out, and several other documents at random, before sealing the sack and taking it to be burnt. The incinerator operator and I each signed the certificate of destruction.

Next evening I put all the stolen documents in my briefcase and went to see Mr Smith. He was surprised at my unscheduled visit, but when I emptied my briefcase on to his desk his eyes nearly popped out of his head.

'Holy moses! It'll take at least two hours to photocopy this lot!'

'Don't bother. You can keep them.'

'Would you mind explaining!'

'Not now. I've got to get back.'

I hoped I had bought myself some American goodwill.

*

Colonel Shalatov had succeeded Misha as head of 7th Division and he wanted to mark his term of office with a really spectacular success. He decided that I should lure the two CIA men, Smith and Mentor, over into East Berlin to meet my husband, the missiles expert. Shalatov himself would impersonate Andrei – until he was ready to arrest them.

The Americans were keen but cautious.

'Couldn't you bring your husband over here to dine with us?'
Mr Mentor said. 'I should have asked him before, but we had
no idea he was in Berlin at all; you've never mentioned it.'

'No. It's impossible for him to cross the border, I'm afraid.
He has too much top secret information.'

'Okay. We'll have him order a new suit – at our expense of
course. One of our people in the East is a tailor, name of
Strelle. Here's the address. Your husband is to go there at five
o'clock next Saturday to be measured.'

Shalatov played his part well. He and Herr Strelle had a long
discussion about the suit, while the tailor's assistant, under
cover of writing down the measurements, photographed my
'husband' from all angles. A date was agreed for the first fit-
ting, and we said goodbye with innocent smiles.

When Ovtshynikov heard that my CIA contacts were to be
pulled in, he decided to break the NWS at the same time. To
them, of course, I was a school-teacher, and the summer holi-
days began on 15 June.

'You will leave for Moscow on the 16th,' the general said,
'and you had better take all your things as it's most unlikely
you'll be coming back. If these two operations are successful,
we won't be able to use you in Berlin again.'

I was startled. Nothing had been said for so long about
letting me go back to Russia, and now I wasn't even sure that I
wanted to go. It would mean seeing Andrei again, and Misha,
and one or other of them would probably demand a decision
from me that I didn't want to make. But the general had more
to say; my personal problems would have to wait.

'Go and see your NWS contacts as soon as possible and ask if
there's anything you can take to Moscow for them. They'll be
delighted.'

They certainly were! Yourka gave me money and leaflets
and a list of addresses. I was aghast.

'Whatever's the use of sending leaflets to Moscow? Don't you
know the penalties for distributing them?'

His eyes glittered with fanaticism. 'Our agents are idealists;
they accept the risks. Most of them are students at the university.'

I packed the stuff in my luggage, wondering how on earth to
get rid of it.

169

Then Shalatov sent me to the Americans to arrange his crucial meeting with Smith and Mentor. They had had the report and photographs from Strelle, and they seemed satisfied that it was worth their while crossing to the East. A date and place were agreed – 20 June at the tailor's shop. I should be safely away by then, and I had to invent some pressing business in Berlin to explain why my husband wasn't travelling with me. Mr Smith wanted to cover every eventuality.

'Just in case we can't make it, would you give your husband this camera. He might have a chance to take a few photographs while he's on vacation.'

He told me the sort of pictures they wanted and handed me a Minox. I listened patiently while he explained how the camera worked, and then put it in my bag beside my own.

There was work I could do in Russia for the CIA too, it seemed; their agent would be getting in touch with me. Smith gave me a cuff-link with a lily engraved on it.

'Our man in Moscow will identify himself by showing you the other one of the pair. Please carry out any instructions he gives you.'

One way and another, it didn't sound as if it would be much of a holiday. I said goodbye to the Americans and went home feeling depressed. I should have been pleased to be leaving a Berlin which had suddenly become so dangerous – but the stranger with the cuff-link would make Moscow dangerous too.

I also knew that I should be forced to choose between Andrei and Misha, and I didn't know whom or what I wanted. I was tired out; sick of the life I was leading; resentful of the way Alik was used to control me. Here in Berlin the free world was so close; somehow he and I must enter it together, before it was too late.

CHAPTER TWENTY-THREE

The Last Journey

Major Arlov drove us to the station in his car. He was going on leave at the same time, and I knew perfectly well that this was no coincidence. He would travel with us, and I would be watched all the way. I was pretty sure, too, that whether I returned to Berlin or not, Alik would be kept in Moscow as a hostage. Ovtshynikov didn't trust me – and he was quite right! The longing to escape had become an obsession.

The Moscow express left at seven, but in accordance with regulations we were there two hours beforehand. Our suitcases were heaved on to the luggage racks and we began settling ourselves into the compartment for the long journey. Alik was over-excited; he was looking forward to seeing his father again. He had a loose milk-tooth which he kept fiddling with, and he was making his gums bleed. I gave him a picture book to try and divert him.

At a quarter past five, Arlov got up.

'I'm just going to get something to read. Won't be long.'

Over at the far side of the station were the stairs to the underground. Every few minutes, a train ran through to the West – to freedom. Why shouldn't I simply run with Alik to those stairs and get away before the major came back. I stood up as casually as I could and looked out of the window. At one end of our carriage was a Soviet guard, and at the other, an East German policeman. Arlov was taking no chances.

Presently he came back with newspapers and a few packs of German cigarettes.

'Funny thing, I've just seen Alfred. He's standing over there by the buffet. Come to see you off, I suppose.'

My heart pounded. Perhaps Alfred could do something to help us. I had to speak to him. But it would be no good getting out of the train unless I could take Alik with me.

The little boy was quietly looking at his book, but all the time his finger was working away in his mouth. Arlov was standing in the corridor. Suddenly, I knew what to do.

'Keep at it, Alik!' I whispered. 'If you can get that tooth out, I'll buy you a present!'

He twisted and wriggled the tooth and got it bleeding nicely. Soon his mouth and his fingers were covered in blood. I got up and called to Arlov.

'Just look at this child! I'll have to take him to the first aid post.'

'Don't worry, I'll go and find an orderly,' Arlov said.

'No – they'll have to put some antiseptic on it. What a nuisance! You'd better stay and look after the luggage.'

All unsuspecting, the major looked at his watch. 'Ten to six; you've got time to have him looked at.'

As we left the train I distributed the blood a little further over Alik's face. The Soviet guard stopped us.

'Where is the Red Cross post?'

He shrugged. 'How should I know? Ask the policeman.'

I didn't have to pretend to be agitated. The policeman directed us to the far corner of the station. I took Alik's hand and tried to hurry him along.

'Come on! I'm going to buy you something nice!'

He wanted to know what it was before he committed himself to a faster pace.

'Oh, anything. You can choose anything you like!'

I was looking desperately for Alfred, the CIA courier who had taken me over to West Berlin so many times. If only he would do it just once more! But he was nowhere to be seen. A Soviet soldier saluted me. God almighty, I was in uniform! I could never get to the West like that. Alik was tugging at my hand; he had seen a kiosk where they sold sweets, fruit, rubber balls – raincoats! He wanted a ball but I insisted on buying raincoats, one each, and an orange for him.

'Here, we'll put these coats on and then we'll look alike. Won't that be fun! Okay?'

He wasn't sure, but I felt a lot safer with my uniform covered. I also realized that I was wasting time looking for Alfred. The stairs to the underground were quite close, and I rushed Alik down them. On the platform, he started to grizzle.

'Look, why don't you eat your orange?'

I peeled it and gave him the segments, one at a time. It seemed ages before a train came in, and when it did, it was crowded. At the border a policeman got on to check the passengers.

'Your identity card, please!'

I swung round, startled, and my elbow hit Alik in the face. He began to cry in earnest. I fumbled in my bag with trembling hands with Alik yelling beside me. The policeman looked at his face, smeared with blood, tears and orange juice.

'It's all right, leave it, lady!'

The train went on. I wasn't sure how soon I could rely on being well away from the checkpoints. Suddenly Alik stopped crying and held up a tiny reddish object.

'Look, mamushka, my tooth! I've got it out!'

I hushed him and talked to him in German, and the poor child looked utterly bewildered.

At Schöneburg I decided we were safe. It was pouring with rain when we reached the street and I couldn't think what to do. I dragged Alik along, splashing through the puddles, and after a time we came to a catholic church with people just going in for the service. I followed them inside; it was a chance to get out of the wet and calm myself, if nothing more. When I knelt to pray, the words, unbidden, came in Polish, a language I hadn't spoken or thought about for years. Alik was very patient, but when the service was over and everyone else was leaving, he shattered my brittle peace.

'When are we going to see papasha?'

'Never, darling, never again!' I broke down and sobbed uncontrollably.

'Is there anything I can do to help you?' The vicar had come quietly up to our pew. I couldn't speak.

'Your little boy is wet through. Let me take you both to the vicarage.'

173

I followed him as if in a dream. In his warm study, he came to help me off with my raincoat. I clutched it, but he had already seen the uniform underneath.

'Please, I'm German, I really am! You must believe me!'

'It doesn't matter,' he smiled. 'If you need help, that's what I'm here for. It doesn't make any difference who you are.'

He took away our dripping coats, and made some tea, and soon I was telling him all about our escape.

'If you would be kind enough to ring this number, and say Jelena Pushkova is here, my friends will come and fetch us.'

But were they my friends? For the first time since leaving the train, I suddenly had doubts. Suppose, after all, they wouldn't help me? And why should they? I was of no further use to them now. Who were my real friends, and, come to that, which side was I really on? I didn't know. All I could be sure of was that I wanted a life, for myself and for my son, where one didn't have to take sides at all, and where the truth wasn't just something else to fear.

When Mr Mentor arrived at the vicarage, he bundled us quickly into his car and drove in silence to CIA headquarters. He got one of the woman officers to take charge of Alik, and then he led me in to face them all. There was no friendliness in his voice as he asked me to explain myself.

'My name is Helga Wannenmacher and I'm a German national.'

There was a moment of consternation. Lieutenant-Colonel Smith was the first to recover.

'The fact that you speak German doesn't prove a thing.'

I spread out all my various identity cards on the table; they didn't prove much, either, except for the red one. I held it up.

'Look! I'm nothing to do with any trade mission; I'm a captain in the KGB!'

'Since when have they had Germans . . . ?'

'Oh, it's too long a story. I'll tell you some other time. The important thing now is – don't go to that meeting with my husband. He's not my husband, he's my boss, and he's planning to arrest you!'

They were really interested now, leaning forward around the table, though I could see that they still didn't quite believe me.

Desperately wondering how to convince them, I remembered something else.

'Mr von Grau must be warned too. They're about to break the NWS.'

'What!' Smith shouted. 'You've worked with them as well?' He turned to one of his officers. 'Get Grau here, at the double!'

Mr von Grau stopped in the doorway and stared at me in astonishment.

'Do you know this woman?'

'Of course I do, she's our best contact.'

'Did you always speak Russian with her?'

'Sure. She doesn't understand German.'

'In that case I have news for you. She *is* German!'

'Why couldn't you have told us?' von Grau asked me, a little peevishly.

'Because there's more to it than that,' Mr Mentor answered for me. He held up my KGB card. 'If she's telling the truth, your people aren't safe. They must move their headquarters immediately and play possum for a while.' Then he turned to me.

'Miss Wannenmacher, you haven't treated us very well, have you? We shall want proof of your good faith before we take things any further. We've started a file on your husband, the missiles expert, and it contains a series of excellent photographs taken in Herr Streele's shop. You say this man is your boss. Tell us exactly who he is!'

I knew that everything depended on my answer, and thanked God it wasn't Misha I was being asked to betray.

'He's Colonel Shalatov, head of 7th Division, KGB.'

'Thank you,' said Mr Mentor gravely, 'I really appreciate that. We'll take care of you and your son.'

Epilogue

During the night of 16 June, 1956, an American Air Force Dakota took off from Templehof Airport in the pouring rain. Alik was fast asleep on my lap; I was slumped in my seat, physically and emotionally exhausted; and the four CIA men with us were tense and quiet. After a time, Lieutenant-Colonel Smith looked at his watch and broke the silence.

'We're just entering West German air space. There's nothing more to fear.' He handed me a cigarette and lit one himself.

'Where are we going?'

'Never mind. To a safe place. We shall have to ask you a great many more questions, I'm afraid; but if you tell the truth, you can have quite a career with us.'

'No! I'll answer your questions, but I'll never, never work for any secret service again!'

'Is that so?' The American narrowed his eyes against the smoke and gave me a searching look. 'We'll see, shall we? "Never" is a dubious word, in any language.'